Federico Amadeo Chiodinari

The Corona Decameron

Adventures of a Foreign Student in Italy

With illustrations by
Miriam Fabbra Fiorentina

Federico Amadeo Chiodinari (alias Friedrich Gottlob Nagelmann) studied law and foreign languages in several civilized European countries as well as in Bavaria. After ten years of apprenticeship in Giovanni Boccaccio's workshop for creative writing in Florence, he escaped unemployment among academics as a teacher at a northern German university of ex-excellency. In addition to scholarly writings on holes in international law, the toolification of European law, and the banana dispute between banana republics, he aims to qualify in the swamp of satire with this volume. Like all academic writings, this booklet is not intended to be read, but seeks to document its author's years of suffering in hopes of reward.

Miriam Fabbra Fiorentina, the author's incomparable daughter, is exploring medicine, music and the world of men after graduating from high school. Thankfully, she has spent an entire Corona month illustrating this book, creating drawings that reflect the content of the stories even better than the stories themselves. The reader in a hurry should therefore look only at the drawings.

To my family

and in memory of Richard Maury,

painter from Florence,

and my cousin Barbara,

who left us way too soon

© 2022 Chiodinari, Federico Amadeo

Language consulting for Austrian German:
Cristina Canneta
Editing and proofreading: Annica Montescuola,
Sofia Solistizia, Geltrude Caronte, Barbara Scellini,
Anna Laura Ferrucci, Susanna Ricciardi,
Tania Del Sindaco, Nora Ermangilda
Technical design: Annabella Gufo

Table of Contents

Table of Contents

Prologue: How it all began

The Black Death came from the Orient, swinging his scythe relentlessly through Puglia, Naples and Rome to the heart of Italy, to the capital of medieval art and poetry, Florence. There he raged terribly, as Boccaccio tells us, claiming innumerable victims among young and old, rich and poor, nobles, clergy, and commoners. People forgot their education, culture and religion and sought only to survive. Neighbors and relatives, even brothers and sisters, husbands and wives, parents and children, all abandoned one another, and greedy, coarse and ponderous men and women were only willing to nurse the sick for a high wage.

Facing death, some retreated to their homes, shunning all contact with the outside world, practicing moderation in eating and drinking, and entertaining themselves with music and other diversions. Others did the exact opposite, gadding around day and night drinking and hooting, from one tavern to another, gratifying every desire, and trying to defy death with laughter, song, and lust.

Others sought their salvation in flight and went to their country estates in the vicinity. Such was the plan of seven young ladies of good family, who chose three respectable young men as their companions for their protection and entertainment. Together they retired with some servants to the Villa Schifanoia, a stately estate in the hills above Florence, with luxuriant gardens and proud avenues of cypresses. There, with games and dances, they spent ten days telling each other stories, ten times ten stories.

Every day, they chose a king or queen among themselves, who chose a great theme. Each of them then had to tell a story. These stories were about sultans and kings, craftsmen, peasants and rogues, and they were set all over the world. Whether they are fine or coarse, tragic or comical, they always reflect the joy of life, humanity and brotherhood. Noblemen, councilors and churchmen come off particularly badly, simple people play on them all kinds of tricks. Thus these stories made a fool of the Black Death and heralded a new world that closed the door to the Dark Ages behind it forever.

A scarce earth-second later, namely after exactly six hundred and forty-seven years, I moved into the Villa Schifanoia. I had not fled the plague, but I had studied law in Bavaria - and understood just enough of it to find it unpleasant. While my studies were still bearable thanks to lots of travel, languages and music, my legal clerkship, the preparatory service with courts, lawyers and in administration, had exhausted the proverbial patience. One was constantly confronted with disputes of intransigent contemporaries, was set to collect other people's money or to justify dubious decisions of the administration. Self-righteous judges and civil servants tried to make you believe that the solutions to social problems in the modern world could be elicited from centuries-old legal texts through legal artistry.

But even worse, I discovered that lawyers in practice have to work a lot and under stress if they don't want to be starvelings. After my cosy student days, I admittedly preferred the appearance of work by far to the work itself, since it messes up your whole day. Therefore, entering into professional practice frightened me terribly. It's obvious: if you're late, life punishes you - and if you've never worked properly until you're thirty, you're no longer good for it, it's definitely too late for you.

It is true that Gerhard Polt, a well-known Bavarian anthropologist of primitive cultures, has made the remarkable suggestion to stem the flood of pensioners that one should bring forward the retirement period at a younger age and then only dare to enter the profession at the age of forty or fifty. Unfortunately, this proposal, like many other innovative ideas, has not yet been able to gain acceptance in our encrusted society.

Therefore, I had no better idea than to escape back into science. There I hoped to do less harm and lead a more pleasant life. That's how I ended up at the Villa Schifanoia. For many years after the days of the Decameron it had housed the papal residence in Florence, but now it had become the seat of an international university, with students from every country in Europe and beyond. Secluded from reality and temporarily relieved of material worries by scholarships, we dealt there with the growing together of the European peoples in economics, law, politics and history.

But more than the research, I was fascinated by sharing my daily life with other Europeans in the equally chaotic and likeable Italian society. Just as Boccaccio described, Italians despise their state and other authorities, but cherish shrewdness, cunning, and sensuality - which is why they elect the country's biggest braggarts, scoundrels, and womanizers as leaders.

Yesterday plague, today Corona: only the new epidemic has led me to collect my Italian stories in a book - as a Corona Decameron, so to speak. Boccaccio may forgive my presumption.

I. Anecdote to lower the morale of the state

„A ticket to the station, please!"

In a foul mood, I boarded the city bus at Florence's *Amerigo Vespucci* Airport late one autumn evening. The Lufthansa had cancelled my flight to Munich at the last minute due to strong winds, and I found myself heading back to the city against my will. Outside, darkness had already fallen, with only the street lamps providing sparse light. The bus drove through the outer quarters of the city with their oversized streets and soulless new buildings, construction sins of the last decades. They would turn in their graves, the masters of the grandiose palaces and churches in the old city! *The death penalty should be abolished, except for architects,* an insight impressively confirmed here, I mused.

Not a soul was waiting at any of the bus stops along the route, so I was to remain the only passenger until the station. The bus was an older-looking Fiat, painted in an ugly orange on the outside and the windows covered with a yellowish layer of dirt, probably desert sand blown from the Sahara. The engine roared so hard that the interior trim kept vibrating along with it, while dirty grey plastic seats and restraining straps were dangling from the ceiling like lianas in a plastic jungle. There was a dubious smell over everything. Not such a successful advertisement for newly arrived tourists, I thought.

"Welcome aboard this latest-series comfort bus," the driver called out, clearly pleased to have a late-evening passenger. Not exactly slim and in his so-called prime, he could have passed for a left-wing intellectual with his horn-rimmed glasses and tangled hair. The impression was not deceiving: next to the driver's seat lay the tattered *Il Manifesto,* the daily newspaper of the Italian Communist Party.

"Where are you from, sir?" inquired the bus driver.

"From Germany, but I've lived here for a few years," I replied indifferently.

A joyful smile flitted across his face, "What a nice coincidence, I lived there for twenty years too, I was a bus driver for Stadtwerke Essen. Yes, Germany, that's a good country, you know, not such a corrupt mess as here."

"But I like it in Italy, the weather is better and the people are friendlier," I tried to brush him off with a few platitudes, because I didn't really feel like having a conversation.

"But you have a functioning state with politicians and authorities who really care about you," he said in a sweeping blow. "If you pay your taxes, then you get something in return. Here the state is a parasite that sucks you dry and drives you crazy with its slow bureaucracy. Nothing works, but still they withhold half of your pay for taxes. And all the time you get fines for things no one knows are illegal."

Taken off guard by this clear-sighted self-portrait, I now bravely tried to counter: "Oh, it's not so rosy in Germany either, we also have a lot of taxes, fines and a stubborn administration."

"But you don't despise your state. Here everyone tries to avoid the state and to cheat it wherever possible. We only work for family and friends, they're the only ones we can rely on. It's always been like that in Italy, we never trusted our government. Because there are always politicians in there who only care about themselves. That's the reason why the country is not really moving forward."

I spontaneously thought of the head of government as the culprit: "But why did you have to vote for Berlusconi? Always at war with the judiciary, only interested in women, and only doing business in his own pocket!

"You're right," the bus driver replied, "he's a bastard, he's ruined the state with his bad example. And on top of that, he's dumbing us down with his television, which is teeming with partisan reporters and naked models. His administration has set the country back years, and now we're paying the bill. You may know, they've sentenced him to many years in prison, but only ever in the first instance; then he dragged out the trials with his armada of lawyers until everything was prescribed barred. That's why he's never ended up behind bars, where he should stay. The other time he had to do only community service at a nursing home. Even he staged that as a show, singing schmaltzy songs to the old folks from his days as an entertainer on cruise ships."

But suddenly there was a loud bang, as if one of the huge tires had burst. Apparently a phantom of the prime minister must have got on at full speed, because the driver immediately turned to him personally: "But no, dear Silvio, please excuse me, what mean stuff I'm talking about: We Italians love you, you make a fool of the state everywhere we'd like to do the same. You don't give a damn about rules and laws, you even write them yourself! And so you go about your business unmolested and have become filthy rich - we like that, it's our dream! "

These words must have soothed Silvio, for the phantom was gone in an instant.

"But it's still a beautiful country, and I like living here," I objected belittlingly.

"Yes, the good Lord, if he exists, has given us a magnificent landscape and a mild climate. And our ancestors, not yet morons like us, have left us magnificent cities and works of art. Take Michelangelo. Sure, he was a bit of a rare gay bird... But how he could paint, what figures he conjured out of the marble with his chisel, truly spectacular! And he lived to be almost ninety, four hundred years ago! Thank goodness he didn't live today, they would have killed him in the hospital sooner!"

Oh dear, I thought, this is turning into a general reckoning, from Michelangelo's David he now jumps straight to the Goliath in the public health system. Once again I tried to rebuff him:

"I haven't had any bad experiences with medical professionals in Italy so far!"

In reality, I avoided visits to doctors there and always did all my check-ups on my home leaves in Bavaria. And when really necessary, I went to pleasant private doctor's practices in Florence, most of which were covered by my German insurance.

"Giuseppe, a friend of mine, of course you don't know him, had a stabbing pain in his breast. He couldn't afford private treatment, so he had to wait for an appointment at the public hospital. Guess how long that took: three months! If he'd had anything serious, I could be visiting him in the cemetery right now!"

"I'm sure cemetery wouldn't be a good choice either, even dead you'd still be dealing with the bureaucracy," I tried to tease him.

He didn't react to this, however, but took the ball straight away: "That's right, bureaucracy is the basic evil of everything, not just in the health system. There are so many complicated regulations for every detail that we are suffocating. Nobody knows them all and manages to respect them. The authorities know this and make you pay for not being able to comply with a lot of it. "

That's almost a legal-economic justification of corruption, I thought, he could write a doctoral thesis about that at our institute. And now came even an example to illustrate it:

"You should try registering a car here sometime. I did that last week when my old Punto went plodge and I had to buy a new one. You have to go to umpteen government offices, queue for hours everywhere, and it ends up costing you a bundle. If you don't want to take a week off work, an agency that does the registration for you is recommended. There it costs even more, but it doesn't take long. Why? Because the agency people grease the palm of the authorities so they don't have to wait! "

Now it dawned on me why no one was interested in my old Polo with German number plates that I had advertised in a flea market magazine. But suddenly the question came to me: "Why did you actually leave Germany and go back?

"Yes, that was the biggest stupidity of my life," he admitted. "But you have to understand, my boss was an idiot, he always got upset about everything. If I was ever five minutes late to the depot in the morning, or even half an hour behind with the bus timetable! It's different here, everyone is happy when a bus comes at all! "

"Well, half an hour's delay isn't so little for a regular bus either, the Germans are a bit sensitive about that," I pointed out.

"In fact, people have put me off there. On the streets and in the squares they just rush past you, stressed out, and let their mouths hang down! And the coffee in the bars is so expensive, you can't drink it at the counter, you always have to sit down right away, and nobody wants to talk to you! That's no life! And then my wife couldn't stand the weather either. Constant rain and in winter always this grey sky, no sun for days on end, it gets you down! "

With a twinkle in his eye, he added, "I'm sure it happened to you the same way, you couldn't stand it in Germany either, or you wouldn't be living here and speaking our language. "

Immersed in the bus driver's lecture, I hadn't even noticed that we had almost arrived at the station. Only when the brightly lit silhouette of the church towers of Santa Maria Novella came into view did I remember that I still hadn't paid.

"I still have to buy the ticket," I remarked dutifully.

"To hell with the stupid transport department that make me drive around here for a pittance on this stinking junk bus," the driver exclaimed, solemnly shaking my hand in farewell and speaking, "My friend, it was nice riding with you, the ride won't cost you anything today!"

There was a deafening hiss, the phantom sparkled once more, and a smug grin settled over his face before slowly dissipating. On the ground, however, it had left a piece of paper. An application for membership of *Forza Italia,* Berlusconi's party.

II. Surprises in Fiesole

Soon after our arrival, I had found an apartment in a beautiful little house near our research institute to share with Stephanie, the best girlfriend of all. This was outside the city in the town of Fiesole, perched like an eagle's nest on a hill high above Florence.

The Fiesolans are a proud people, who derive directly, as indeed nothing worth mentioning has happened in the meantime, from the Etruscans, who lived in the area three thousand years ago. The Fiesolans use to look down on the hickish inhabitants of the Arno valley below them in the truest sense of the word. After all, Florence was built on barren marshes that had only been drained recently, namely in the 11th century AD.

Shortly after our arrival, an election poster of the mayor of the communist party announced the daring pride of the Fiesolans. Framed by hammer and sickle, it depicted a dignified elderly gentleman in a tailor-made suit, and next to him, in large letters, was an election slogan that followed quite casually from the Communist doctrine: *So that we may continue to live better!* Marx, Engels and Lenin, but perhaps also Don Camillo and Peppone, would have been delighted.

Our landlady had built our little house from an old stable building and an orangery next to her villa. It was surrounded by an enchanted garden with olive and persimmon trees, in which the remains of building materials and old woods were gathering. Surely it would all come in handy someday, the old crone always mumbled. High stone walls lined the garden on three sides, and a massive metal gate closed the entrance to the street. So we could feel safe - at least until one Tuesday evening in early December. As we painfully learned, it's not just businessmen who are in high demand in the run-up to Christmas, but also other, unjustly less respected professions.

"You left the window open, darling," Stephanie noted in surprise as we returned after shopping at the supermarket. Although it was only about five in the evening, it was already getting dark. Our house had part window bars, part armor-like metal blinds, but we hadn't closed them in our haste.

"Someone must have opened the window," Stephanie now cried out in horror. Indeed, the oak front door was locked tight as a castle, but the large window next to it was open a crack. Without really grasping the situation, I briskly unlocked the door, and we were standing in the entryway that spilled into the living room. The whole thing presented an awful sight: The furniture was out of place, the cupboards open and ransacked. An uninvited guest must have paid us a visit.

"We need to look upstairs in the bedroom," it came to me. There were our laptops with our work on them, a camera, money, and what little jewelry we could buy with the scholarships.

"You, maybe they're still up there, I'm scared, I'm not going up there," Stephanie stammered. We froze with fear, listened strained, but could not hear any sounds from above. Then I had the idea of getting our English neighbor Murray to help.

Mr. Murray was a theologian and philosopher, and also worked at the Institute, but he had been taken out of research and disposed of in a high administrative position. He was known for his good-natured manner, savvy with alcohol, and his hopelessly dysfunctional relationship with the language of his host country. When I knocked, he immediately opened the door and helpfully asked, "Hello darling, is there anything wrong with you?"

We reported that we had found the house open and everything pointed to a visit from burglars.

"Indeed, I've heard a big bang half an hour ago or so, I thought you had crashed a bottle of wine, it has just happened to me as well, you know," he confirmed amiably.

"Yeah, but maybe the thieves are still here," Stephanie replied shakily.

Fortunately, Mr. Murray was also a Jesuit, and so his theological convictions did not keep him from an active peace mission. To this end, he unceremoniously grabbed an antiquarian poker in front of the open fireplace and rushed up the oak stairs like a berserker with his artificial hip. Gratefully, I ran after him, but could barely keep up. While still running he yelled, "Is there anyone up there?", firmly believing that Italian hoodlums spoke fluent English. Not so far-fetched in view of the masses of tourists, I thought.

Of course, no one was upstairs anymore, but we found everything ransacked there as well. Our modest stashes of money, the camera and Stephanie's jewelry were missing - especially an elegant silver ring with a ruby set into it. The goldsmith Vittorio, the brother of a southern Italian friend, had made it for us. Stephanie wore it only on special occasions; it was her showpiece. Was, indeed it was, which was dreadful. The older laptops had been left by the thieves, apparently in realistic appreciation of the scientific thought stored on them. Lucky, that could have taken weeks of work, I thought, as the backups were in a messy state.

Our neighbor said a comforting goodbye, "please let me know if I can do anything else for you, darling," and we slowly regained our composure.

"In any case, we have to call the police, we should have done that immediately," I said. I courageously called 112.

"Carabinieri," came a voice on the other end of the line. I started to describe the circumstances of the burglary - who, when, where, what etc., as one is taught in primary school, learning goal accident reporting.

But the voice abruptly interrupted me, "Are the thieves still in the house?"

"Of course not," I replied brusquely, "or I wouldn't be sitting here so calmly calling you."

"Then what do you want with us?" the policeman inquired impatiently.

"I thought you were coming by to visit the crime scene and pick up clues," I interjected in my defense.

"Forget it. We don't investigate thefts, where should we start? But if you need a certificate, then simply come to the police station in the next few days and make a report, the colleagues have forms ready for the authorities and insurance companies. If you don't have insurance, you can forget about it, because nothing will come of it anyway. And now I'm afraid I'll have to throw you off the line, because people with serious problems might call. Good evening, then," the carabiniere concluded the conversation and immediately hung up.

We sat perplexed in the confusion of our living room and looked at each other. It was one of those moments in earthly existence when intellectuals, especially scientists, who go through life with proper rationality and sobriety, should say to themselves, the important thing is that you are healthy and unharmed. And the thieves didn't kidnap you and chain you in a Sardinian earth cave for a couple of months in winter, until the ransom was paid, if the family could even raise that much cash. Or they didn't stab you between the ribs prematurely and then dissolve the carcass in acid in the old Camorra tradition. And anyway, people in other countries are exposed to much worse criminality, which, by the way, can also be statistically proven, as our sociologist colleague Daniele has shown in his latest publication... In the end, we can be grateful to the thieves that they only took the jewelry....

"I could really despair about that ring," Stephanie abruptly interrupted my musings, "we can't get it back, it had such a personal touch, I designed it myself with Vittorio; and now we don't have the money to have a new one made. Vittorio said the other day that the prices of rough stones are now prohibitive."

I imagined the thief putting our ring on his girlfriend's finger, and that sent me into intemperate rage. Lost in thought, I let my eyes wander aimlessly around the living room. Furniture was scattered throughout the room, and the sofa barricaded the entrance to the kitchen. At least the rustic china cabinet made of poplar wood, which our landlady had deposited here due to lack of space in her villa, was still in its place. Because of its huge weight, it could not be moved so easily.

But suddenly I saw something strange flashing under the cabinet. I approached, bent down, and incredulously saw a kind of rod, or rather a chisel made of metal that had already started to rust in places. As a crime spectator trained from my youth, I immediately deduced: the thieves used this to pry open the window, you can even see that the frames are bent. When the frame then gave way with a thud, the chisel slipped away and slid under the cabinet, and they didn't find it there. Or maybe they were in a hurry and could only take the stolen goods. In any case, Inspector Montalbano would have been delighted with me for having such a pronounced criminal acumen, which I am sure is rare among laymen, I thought.

"Now we lash them into a frenzy," I triumphed, "even the lax Italian police must have collections of fingerprints with which to match the marks on the chisel. And since our thieves have certainly broken in somewhere else, chances are the police have their prints stored and know right away who to arrest. If we're lucky, our stuff's still there, too. I'm sure the thieves weren't careful enough to use gloves."

I was, though. I dug my woolen gloves out of the dresser in the bedroom, used them to get the chisel out from under the cabinet, and carefully slid it into a freezer bag, which I tied carefully. This was what professional forensics looked like! Only idiots would have taken a used plastic bag here, I thought, because there would be other traces in it with which the fingerprints could mix beyond recognition. With this bag, I set off for the nearest police station without further delay.

So I drove my old Polo up the hill to Fiesole and rang the bell at the Carabinieri gate at about eight o'clock in the evening. It was all barred, only in the middle a peephole allowed a look inside.

Over the intercom I introduced myself as a German student living here and described my request. A younger policeman opened the door and called out to me mischievously: "You're lucky that someone is still here, the colleagues are all gone, because tonight Fiorentina is playing against Bologna, we absolutely have to win.

In the reception room hung a monumental painting showing a policeman from Fiesole. He looked as strong as a bear, but an SS officer held him at bay with a rifle. Under the latter's eyes, in contempt of death, he dug his own grave, into which he would soon be thrown in retaliation for partisan attacks on German troops, with a few bullets in his chest.

"Those are bygone days, thank goodness," the policeman placated when he sensed my trepidation looking at the picture, "Thank goodness we now have a united Europe and only fight each other in football. Which team do you support, Bayern Munich perhaps? - But I'm sure you have a problem you want to tell me," he continued, instilling confidence.

Thus encouraged, I described the burglary that had occurred and explained that I needed a copy of the report for the insurance company. Triumphant over my criminalistic acumen, I then placed the thief's tool in the freezer bag in front of him on the office desk. To remove the chisel, of course, I used my woolen gloves again. However, as they were much too thick, I only got hold of the metal after a few attempts.

The policeman noted this with amusement and said with a pitying look at me: "We'll save the trouble of taking the minutes for the insurance company, I'll just give you the confirmation signed and stamped by me to take home, and you describe on it the course of events and enter the stolen items - truthfully, of course," he added with a wink. "The insurance company won't care anyway, since it's a small claim."

"And as for this rusty junk here," he spoke piquedly, turning to the chisel with feigned disgust, "if I had ever seen it and you had officially turned it in to me, which of course you haven't, I would have to confiscate it immediately, for it is the tool of a crime. But we already have two basement rooms full of such things, which we can rarely attribute to a criminal, but instead auction off every few years and throw the rest away. That's why I advise you to take the thing back with you, then at least you'll have a chisel now." Conspiratorially, he whispered to me, "And if you ever accidentally lock yourself out, now you know what to do. "

I capitulated, bowed silently to the painting in the reception room and left the station dejectedly with the policeman. When he saw my sad face, he obviously wanted to cheer me up a bit as a farewell and asked: "Do you actually also have jokes about us policemen in Germany?"

"No, not a single one," I replied, "for they are all true!"

III. Amanda or the birth of a new language

Amanda was a Spanish fellow student in her mid-twenties, with jet-black hair, striking features and sparkling eyes. She had a sunny disposition and was always up for adventure and banter. Unlike most southern European women at the Institute, she dressed casually and was not tarted up, which made her likeable in my eyes. In Santiago de Compostela she had studied history and cultural studies, but thanks to the Erasmus exchange program she had been in Austria for a longer period of time and therefore spoke good German - a peculiar German with a few mistakes, but a lovely sound and a coloring that only an Austrian Galician can have.

Undoubtedly, as she once recounted, a handsome Austrian naturalist was not entirely innocent of her German. Going beyond the intentions of its inventors, Erasmus leads not only to purely study-related but also to more holistic encounters among European peoples (which is why in student jargon the *er is* also replaced by *org* - meaning, of course, the domain extension).

In Florence, Amanda wrote a doctoral thesis on cultural and local associations of Galicia. This field of research revealed an attractively liberal side of our institute: In the history department, they allowed all kinds of topics for doctorates, even those for which there were no sources in Florence. That is why the West Indian Tea Company, decolonization in Africa and English propaganda against Nazi Germany were represented just as much as the salon life of Toulouse-Lautrec in 19th-century Paris, historical museums in European comparison or Galician regional culture. To study the sources, the doctoral students then undertook field trips home, for which they received extra grants to supplement their stipends.

Inspiration and imagination were the driving forces of the historians, who were absorbed in their past universes during the day and in the student bar Fiasco every evening. Amanda gave a taste of this when I once saw her coming out of the history department. She had chosen the *History of Political Scandal* seminar over competing courses on *Romantic Love in European History* and *Libido and the Law in the European Union.*

"Hello Amanda," I greeted her, "are you creating another scandal today?"

"A Frenchwoman gave a presentation on the scandal of Queen Marie Antoinette's collar, you know, that was still before the French Revolution".

"I've never heard of her collar," I objected, "I can only imagine she didn't enjoy it that long."

"Well, are you going to make fun of me, you fool?" she scoffed.

"I would never do that to a budding historian," I defended myself. But then another doubt came to me: "I didn't know you spoke French too, Amanda, my compliments!"

"I don't actually know a word," she confessed.

"What, but you've just been to a seminar in French?"

"Well, I understand a lot through Spanish, and the rest I simply imagine..."

This innovative approach to *mental history,* which has not yet received the attention it deserves in the discipline, left me in awe.

A few days later, I met Amanda walking in the hills behind Fiesole. She was not alone, however, but embraced a red-haired giant of decidedly Nordic origin intimately. Naturally, my suspicions immediately fell on the nature-boy from the Alpine country. The giant didn't necessarily shine with his beauty, but that's not what counts with us men, as a well-known Austrian saying confirms: *When a man is more beautiful than a monkey, that's a luxury!*

So I immediately greeted Amanda's appendage in German, "Pleased to meet you, I've heard a lot about you."

Amanda was visibly embarrassed: "Excuse me, it's not what you think, I thought you'd met before, that's Leif from Sweden, he's in the History Department, we're together now."

Communication then proved to be problem-free, however, because Leif also spoke good German - only not with an Austrian accent, but a dark Nordic one, which, to say the least, exuded a little less Mediterranean eroticism than that of his partner.

Nevertheless, Amanda and Leif stayed together. And since she didn't speak English very well, not to mention Swedish, and he didn't speak Spanish either, they conducted their relationship in a language that is actually not popular, even discredited as difficult, and familiar to most Europeans only from Nazi films: in German. Leif was in no hurry to get his doctorate, he had already been researching Swedish film history for five years and was working as a professor's assistant. That's why Amanda finished her doctorate much earlier, and when her scholarship expired, he moved back to Santiago with her. Since university posts were also scarce in Spain, Amanda had to make do with a job teaching Galician and history at a grammar school. Leif got a job as a lecturer at a Swedish correspondence university, so he was able to spend most of the year in Santiago.

Some time after their return to Spain, Amanda gave birth to a son who, despite his southern name of Pablo, took after his father in appearance and complexion.

"When he was still a new-born baby," she told me later, "the pediatricians in the hospital worried about him, because he looked so pale. One of the doctors even wanted to put him under the heat lamp so that he could get a bit of color - 'he must have something wrong with his skin,' he said. But when the midwife came in, she laughed at everyone and said: 'Gentlemen, you haven't seen the father yet'." A little later, he entered the room, and all the doctors heaved a sigh of relief.

Amanda was also to get into trouble with the authorities with her son. On the way back from her first visit to her Swedish parents-in-law, the police stopped her at the identity check at the airport and made a serious accusation: "Even though I presented them with the correct identity papers, they didn't believe that I was the mother of this pale rascal there; they accused me of having stolen him in Sweden. It took a call to the father to allay the suspicions of the dutiful border officials.

In the meantime I visited Amanda and Leif once in Santiago. Pablo was already five years old and had been joined by a little sister named Conchita. Amanda and Leif continued to speak German among themselves, while the children obviously understood everything but preferred to speak Spanish. However, their German had developed a considerable Austro-Swedish-Galician life of its own and was increasingly becoming the couple's private language. Although I, as a Bavarian, am reasonably fluent in German, I no longer understood everything. Linguists in two thousand years will not be envious of the task of scientifically clarifying the origins of the German dialect spread among pale-skinned people in northern Spain, which deviates from the standard language to the point of unrecognizability.

"This is Federico, a friend of ours from Italy", Amanda introduced me to her family after my arrival, "you have to pay respect to him, he is now a big shot at a university in northern Germany, not so far away from Sweden. Ah, and now he's got a gin trap on his finger," she gurgled with thieving joy, her eyes fixed on my wedding ring. "And look, on his snout he has no longer the snappy sportsman's specs from earlier, but golden professor's glasses, which is supposed to show intelligence and a bit more diligence, I guess?"

"That's not a snout," Pablo interjected in Spanish, " the elephants we saw at the zoo the other day have snouts. But my dad has one too, you only see it in the bathroom, and he wears it further down."

Leif looked at him uncomprehendingly, and from his look spoke the expression of deep regret, as if he wanted to say: My dear son, I don't understand you, unfortunately I don't speak your language. Leif then asked in German, "What funny things are you telling our guest there, Pablo?"

Pablo sputtered out in a Spanish torrent of words, from which I thought I heard some of the curses that are now elevated standard in European kindergartens.

Addressing me, Pablo expertly explained, "You have to know, my dad always speaks so funny, you can't understand him, all my friends laugh. My mom says he's just too stupid to speak Spanish, but he's still a good person."

IV. Kim the Third

With Americans I had not yet had much to do, just as a generation before me Gerhard Polt said about the Russians that he had only sparse contact with them, because back then people mainly used to shoot each other. Of course I knew that the Americans, as the leading world power, wanted to bring democracy, freedom and hamburgers to the other nations and, thanks to superior military technology, could not only strike anywhere at any time, but also liked to exchange bullets among themselves frequently and gladly.

For, as even the Constitution guarantees, every American is allowed to bear arms in order to better fight the enemy at home, in marriage, in the family, at school, at university and at work. And in these places, as we know, are many enemies.

A first encounter took place while I was still a teenager with an exchange student of my brother from Cincinnati who spent some time with my family in Bavaria. Since he didn't speak much, I only learned that he was about to graduate in Greek mythology, breaststroke, trumpet, and vivisection of insects. When he left us again after a few weeks, he had become intensively acquainted with the girls from the neighborhood and of the German language at least with the important expressions *Guten Tag, Danke* and *Auf Wiedersehen.*

At the beginning of my stay at the Institute, Greg, a visiting American researcher, did his bit for the reputation of the world's leading power. As soon as he arrived, he reported: "You know, I have just been to Florence downtown this morning, and I have seen all of it, and now I am going to Venice for the rest of the day..." On another occasion, we arranged to meet in the evening in a larger group in the center, specifically in Piazza Santa Croce. This square is one of the architectural highlights of Florence. The Franciscan Basilica of Santa Croce, with its neo-Gothic façade, is enthroned in the middle of the square; famous people from the history of humanity such as Dante, Michelangelo, Galileo and Rossini are buried there. Both flanks and the back of the square are adorned with grandiose palazzi of various periods. When we asked Greg, "Do you want to join us in Piazza Santa Croce tonight?" he just made sure to ask, "Do you mean in the church or on the parking lot in front of it?"

The bright spots, on the other hand, and this brings me at last to the real story, were the exchange students from American universities who always visited the Institute for one or two semesters. In my second year such glimpses were particularly rewarding, for three decidedly good-looking women from California, New York, and Chicago had come to Florence. Since the English language is apparently stingy with female first names, or perhaps because relations with North Korea were even better at the time, all three had the same name, *Kim*.

After weeks of awkward misunderstandings, a distinction began to emerge in the conversations among us: Kim I from New York had ancestors from Kerala and a mysterious dark face, which earned her the name *Indian Kim*. Kim II from Chicago was a blonde beauty of Scandinavian descent. Since she was otherwise unremarkable, she was given the not-so-witty name *Kimberley-Kim*. Finally, Kim III from California was a stunner of a woman, quick-witted and always in a good mood. Although she looked perfect, which must have been hard for her to miss over the years, she was not one bit arrogant. Some of her ancestors came from Romania, she once told me, and indeed she would not have cut a bad figure as a Balkan princess.

It is a truth universally acknowledged that a bachelorette on a good scholarship must be in want of a man, and thus in a short time Kim III acquired a male fan club from various countries. The quirk of tossing her head sideways in a graceful turn and running her fingers through her shiny brown-black hair became her onomastic fate. A cynical admirer linked her to a hair shampoo commercial seen on Berlusconi television and dedicated the name *Shampoo-Kim to* her. Although not very nice, it lasted throughout the year.

Over the next few months, Kim III's fan club was to be reduced to a selection of promising admirers, of which I was unfortunately not one. However, Paolo, a classic *Latin lover*: tall, black-haired, with a swarthy face and moustache, had advanced into the illustrious circle. With elegant clothes and distinguished manners, he seemed to have stepped out of the film version of Tommasi di Lampedusa's Leopard.

His story made waves at the institute. Paolo was pursuing a strategy of conquest that was as romantic as it was musical and sporty. Inspired by a custom common on the northern side of the Alps, the "Fensterln" (climbing into the window of one's beloved), he wanted to give Kim an amorous serenade with guitar accompaniment outside her room in the evening, in the hope that the window and more would soon be opened to him.

His repertoire included not only opera classics (*To love one is to betray others* and *E in Spagna mille tre*), but also pieces by the Beatles and the Stones - something should appeal to Kim III's taste! Paolo had already demonstrated his musical abilities in the student bar, winning the hearts of numerous female listeners, but after nightly test runs, he spurned them again. His venture was complicated by the fact that Kim lived on the third floor of a student residence and her window could only be sung to from a relatively steep roof in front of it.

It was a balmy May evening when Paolo planned to put his plan into action. Armed with his guitar and a borrowed climbing rope, he and a few helpers, including myself, drove to Kim's dorm around half past ten. An earlier inspection of the place had shown that it was possible to get into the unlocked attic directly from the stairwell, where there was an easy-to-open glass skylight next to the chimney. Up to there we penetrated fast also this evening. With the help of a bed frame pushed under the hatch, Paolo was then able to climb out quickly.

"The roof isn't that steep, I don't need a rope," he sounded. But the old roof tiles, covered with moss, did not inspire confidence. That's why we advised Paolo: "Come on, don't be careless, tie the rope somewhere and then tie it around you."

"All right, it can't hurt," he replied, fixing one end of the rope to the chimney and looping the other around his chest, expertly secured with a fireman's knot. The rope was part of a mountaineering kit and measured about fifteen meters, which Paolo probably underestimated. When he tied on with it, there was still a larger piece left dangling freely on the roof. Not exactly professional, I thought.

We handed him his guitar and Paolo quickly got over the few meters to Kim's window, where he crouched down. As an intellectual who tried to impress women with profound conversations about the meaningfulness of human existence (which is why I remained single for a long time), one might well find such a situation embarrassing. Not so Paolo, who immediately intoned *O sole mio in* a languorous voice: "How beautiful is a sunny day, the clear air after a storm! The fresh air is like a feast", only to immediately become clearer: "There is no sun more beautiful than you. Oh, my sun shines from You, shines from You, shines from You..."

Kim noticed the singing right away, opened the window and called out to him, "Oh Paolo, is it really you, how lovely, what a great idea, you are a genius, Paolo, really."

Flattered by this compliment, Paolo took another step towards the window, but now events came thick and fast: The roof tile on which his weight rested broke from its moorings, and as a result Paolo slipped away and fell on his rump. Unfortunately, he could not hold on to the slippery roof and slid down the slope, taking several more tiles with him.

"Hold on to the rope," we yelled in horror, but it was already too late - Paolo reflexively clutched his guitar, therefore had no hand free in a hurry and slid further and further until he tumbled down over the edge of the roof. Now, finally, the rope tightened around Paolo's chest with a brutal jerk, causing his still-held guitar to slip away from him and land in a bush below. Paolo came to a stop about three feet below the gutter and was now dangling from the rope, which fortunately was well secured to the chimney.

After a few moments of stupor, Paolo tried to pull himself back up by the rope. But then the gutter over which the rope ran broke from an anchorage, lowered, and more roof tiles crashed to the ground just past Paolo's head.

Startled by the noise, the caretaker, Mr. Bonnini, and some students now came running into the garden. They stared in disbelief at Paolo, who was still hanging from the rope below the edge of the roof. Mr. Bonnini called out excitedly, "Don't move, I'll bring the big ladder, it's safer."

And so Paolo held out on the rope for several more minutes amid the rising mockery of the increasingly numerous spectators. Finally the caretaker found the right one for the tool shed in his legendary plastic bag full of keys and took out a long ladder from it. Arriving on the scene, he wedged its various elements together until a sufficient height was reached. When he then leaned the ladder against the wall of the house next to Paolo, he immediately managed to get both feet on one rung. But now the fireman's knot had to be untied, which had been tightened even more by the fall. Only when this was done was Paolo able to descend, accompanied by the derisive applause of the spectators. Once at the bottom, he complained of chest pains. However, this was to turn out to be a harmless bruised rib, which only left a few black and blue marks.

The next day, Paolo received a promising envelope from Kim III at Bar Fiasco. Inside, however, was not a love letter, but a nice card with flowers and get-well wishes, the kind you send to a rich aunt in the hospital after a kidney stone operation.

Over the next few months, it wasn't Paolo who won the race, but a racy Danish political scientist named Magnus - a Leonardo di Caprio type, only less dandyish, more intelligent and prettier than the original. Kim III picked him out of the circle of her suitors and later even married him.

As her departure from Florence approached, she remembered Paolo again and brought him a gift to the Bar Fiasco, beautifully wrapped in Florentine paper with an elegant cross pattern. With great sympathy from the students present, she handed it to Paolo, who opened it immediately. What emerged was a T-shirt with a writing and a black drawing above it. It showed a thickly bespectacled student in a library, who was only able to peek out from behind the high stacks of books on his desk with difficulty. The books were literally up to his head. Beside him, a puny sparkle burned, providing the light for his nightly studies and giving the whole scenario a touch of *In the Name of the Rose.* But the writing under the drawing read: *Every night spent with a woman is a book not read!* Dare somebody say that Americans are cultureless.

V. Of the little souls of our gardens

The *piccole anime da giardino,* the little souls of our gardens, are fixed points of rest in the otherwise restless occidental civilization. They tend our flowers, shrubs and trees, watch over our driveway avenues, garden castles, ornamental ponds, tool sheds, garages and garbage houses. They always attract curious glances from admirers and passers-by, at whom they sometimes even wolf-whistle thanks to innovative software.

In recent decades, unfortunately, humans have eradicated their formerly mythical existence and degenerated them into special offers in DIY stores. And the quarrelsome way people treat each other also shapes their relationship to the garden souls, which in Germania are lovelessly degraded to garden dwarfs and sent into exile in drab terraced house front gardens. Even graceful gnomes alone could not prevent the German writer Wladimir Kaminer from having to vacate his plot in a Berlin allotment garden, where he had tolerated *spontaneous vegetation* in gross violation of the regulations.

In Italy, despite their affectionate names, the little souls of the gardens are less common. An exception was our neighbor Mrs. Zelmira, by the way a name as melodious as Kunigunde, Walburga or Wiltrud in German. Mrs. Zelmira lived one street away and was a state-certified piano teacher, but because of her advanced age she taught only a few students. Decades ago she had spent some years in Austria for her education, was therefore fond of the German language and liked to talk to us at the garden wall.

From Austria, she once told, she had also brought her dear little garden souls. In the middle of a bewitchingly fragrant herb garden, surrounded by sage, lavender, oregano, thyme and rosemary, she had set up a miniature castle with a pale-skinned beauty known from fairy tale literature. Of whose charms a mirror of desires, as it is called in Italian, boasted quite insubordinately, and thus strongly annoyed the queen of the land. Surrounded by seven little souls with caps and long white beards, the beauty was soon to eat an apple from biodynamic agriculture and perish. Especially the children of the neighborhood liked to stop in front of this ensemble. In addition, admirers from the four-legged population also found themselves there to pursue their love and fecal life.

The disaster occurred out of the blue on a Sunday before Whitsun. During a walk we met a strange gathering of people in front of Mrs. Zelmira's house. The old teacher stood behind her garden wall with a petrified expression, where dwarfish abysses opened up: all the little souls had disappeared without a trace, and next to the miniature castle someone had hung up a pamphlet on two small wooden sticks, which read:

Garden gnomes also possess a soul, even if simple-minded and unscrupulous fellow citizens still do not want to admit it! Unfortunately, unscrupulous people without compassion keep the gnome souls imprisoned in plaster bodies and abandon them to enslavement in evergreen gardens in order to dominate nature, to appropriate venerable fairy tales for themselves and to live out the perversions of a globalized fantasy without restraint. How would you feel in their place - bound in a plaster corset, forced to smile all the time, in snow, rain and cold, mocked and violated by dogs and far away from your home? Don't forget, countless dwarves, an estimated twenty million in Germany alone, are subjected to these torments every day. Yet your statues of dwarfs are nothing but mean idols of capitalism, a standard of those who no longer ask themselves what is true and false in the world, but allow themselves to be lulled into a pleasing illusory world, disfigured by the kitsch of a broad mass and the myth of an eternally green childhood - a Disneyland in kit form for unscrupulous capitalist philistines!

We are a group of militant volunteers who have joined together in the Movimento Autonomo per La Liberazione delle Anime da Giardino (MLAG), the autonomous liberation front of garden souls, to wage a silent but all the more effective battle against the colonization of the human imagination. At night our commandos become active and take garden gnomes into their power. The gnomes then remain hidden in a secret place for a few days until their soul can escape and thus elude the human slavers forever...

Poor Ms. Zelmira, who knew little about these remarks, had not expected such an ideological broadside. A discussion ensued among the passers-by about whether the criticism of garden dwarfs as symbols of the decline of Western civilization was justified - or whether it was simply left-wing buffoons in the mood for provocation who were spreading their folly. Some Berlusconi supporters suspected that, as always, the Communist Party was behind it.

The action of the autonomous liberation front was also reported by a local rag, in which an ambitious journalist tried to link the dwarf robbery to the opponents of globalization and the riots in Genoa on the occasion of the G8 summit. A letter to the editor helpfully suggested that the activists should shoot the Italian NATO bases with bows and arrows for his sake, put the Vatican up for sale on Ebay or just randomly blow up the next best of Silvio's sex parties, but not deprive the old woman of her joy in the garden gnomes.

In protest, or simply because she knew nothing else to do, Mrs. Zelmira left everything as the dwarf liberators had done. The pamphlets remained hanging over the deserted fairy castle.

We were about to forget about it when a few days later, on a Sunday morning, Guido, the eight-year-old son of another neighbor, came running breathlessly to tell everyone that the dwarfs had reappeared. That morning, a walker had spotted them in the nearby Villa Ventaglia city park, gathered in chipper company, as it were, having an aperitif before a bourgeois lunch. A pamphlet also towered above this arrangement:

Our souls have now fled from our human slavers - reduced to lifeless husks, we can now return to their front yards.

After Mrs. Zelmira got her dwarfs back, she put an end to the Snow White installation in her herb garden. She assigned the little souls a new place in her living room on the bookcase, directly above an old book bound in pigskin. This told the dwarves about former MLAG members, namely a Spanish nobleman and his servant, who even took on giants with his aged horse - though not in search of a new social order, only an aloof woman. By all accounts, the dwarves nevertheless enjoyed themselves in this new environment.

On a visit to Mrs. Zelmira's house a few days later, I discovered small holes in the back of all the dwarfs that had been unsightly drilled into them. After a few moments of perplexity, it dawned on me: that must be where the activists had created openings to allow the souls of souls to escape undetected by their human slave masters. It also explained why the dwarves now harmonized casually with the petit-bourgeois living room decor.

The escaped souls have been living among us ever since and have found a new home in the shows of Berlusconian television. Before moving into a retirement home, Mrs. Zelmira gave the soulless dwarf shells to a German tour group she had met in the old town. They are currently in the gardens of various Brandenburg day-care centers, except for the leader, who made it to Vladimir Kaminer's Garden of Eden in Gluglitz.

VI. Night on Earth in Fiesole

„What, I'm supposed to be dangerous and you carry guns?", the taxi driver shouted angrily at a police control who had stopped him - just because he was wearing sunglasses on a hellish drive through the narrow streets of Rome at night, constantly shouting curses at other drivers and driving the wrong way down one-way streets. As a passenger, he had picked up a clergyman who was gasping for breath and apparently suffering from heart problems. The prostitutes and transvestites on the side of the road suggested that he had had himself picked up from a brothel.

The taxi driver took the situation as an opportunity to finally make a confession, namely about his twisted love life. He had started it with ripe pumpkins and later transferred it to a peaceable younger sheep, which his father unfortunately took to the butcher when the affair was discovered, whereupon he had to make do with his sister-in-law - but all only sins of love, as he convincingly argued in his defense. Thus the real Roberto Benigni in *Night on Earth.*

Although the *setting* at the institute was not quite as exciting (not *night on earth,* but *days in the library*), we were also able to come up with our Roberto Benigni - a diminutive lawyer who even resembled the real actor in appearance. The mischievousness was pouring out of his eyes. Outwardly camouflaged with the disdainful matter of European administrative law, he too was entangled in the trials and tribulations of love.

One day we arranged to meet for coffee on the cafeteria terrace. Like a film set, it was framed with ancient statues and afforded a magnificent view of the hills of the Apennines. Roberto told us that he had written an autobiographical short story and submitted it to a magazine readers' contest. It was about the phenomenon of Italian mama's boys who, for convenience, but often also because of high rents, stay in the Hotel Mama until their marriage at the age of about forty-seven, or forever in the absence of one. However, the parental home is sacred, and so they have to meet their girlfriends elsewhere, in the woods, in caves and quarries in the hills of Fiesole or, more contemporary, in Papa's car in parking lots. For their logistical support, thanks to the flexibility of the Italian labor market, the precarious profession of "car tapers" has formed. In many of the city's parking lots, they are on the spot and quickly tape off your car with old newspapers. The cost is one euro, but the later removal is not included in the price.

For fear of being recognized, Roberto opted for a highway parking lot outside Florence, where unfortunately the said service was not available. Moreover, in order to be seen in time by the approaching trucks, Roberto had to leave the parking lights on, which is said to have attracted interested passers-by. Because of these rather adverse circumstances, he said, the meeting as a whole suffered somewhat. And his girlfriend Eliana had always repeated what nonsense they were doing here, and if her mother saw her now, and in general she would never marry such a fool, she would rather enter a convent or go straight to Berlusconi.

Roberto had just finished this story when Serena, Anastasia and Irene entered the terrace with a coffee mug and sat down on a bench near us. Serena was an Italian historian, Anastasia a Greek political scientist, and Irene a German economist. With their winning looks, wide-cut blouses and tight-fitting jeans, they made an electrifying sight.

"Who is this angelic being?" asked Roberto, his eyes imperceptibly pointing to the blonde beauty on the far left.

"This is Irene from the Economy Department," I explained, "she is, as far as I know, writing a doctoral thesis on rent control in residential tenancies."

"I beg your pardon, you've got to be kidding," Roberto replied, "not a single landlord wants rent control, I can't talk to her about it. All right, my administrative law isn't necessarily any more exciting. But why does such a good-looking woman waste her time on scientific nonsense anyway, I'd rather imagine her on a yacht, enjoying drinks in a bikini. But do you know anything else about her, does she have a boyfriend?" he insisted impatiently.

"No, I don't know, she hasn't been here long," I rebuffed. "I've only seen her once at a party, she was with a friend."

"That's really silly that I'm only meeting her now, she's got a cracking figure, I wouldn't, how do you say, push her off the edge of the bed. Couldn't you introduce me, say, as a lawyer and literary writer?"

"That's not good now that she's with the others," I answered, "it looks like a pickup line right away, you better talk to her in the bar when she's alone. "

"There's nothing we can do, that's it, it's too late now," Roberto resigned. And casually he added: "Actually, I came here to tell you something else: on Sunday in a week you are all invited to celebrate, Eliana and I are getting married."

Postscript:

Since Roberto was an atheist who had often made his dislike of religion known, he only married in church for the sake of his wife. After the wedding the priest read out the blessings of none other than the Pope, which a cunning friend had ordered secretly. And since Roberto always proclaimed loudly that he would lead a modern, naturally childless marriage, Eliana bore him a son after only one year, who seemed to take after his father. He was also present at Roberto's oral doctoral examination and, to the astonishment of all present, remained quiet as a mouse. His father only acknowledged this uncomprehendingly: "You unlucky fellow, you should have started crying at the right moment.

VII. The end of Bavarian piracy

It is only natural that we had to recover from the studies at the institute, which were equally exhausting for body and mind, in order to be fit again for the great deeds to come. We especially liked to go sailing on the various seas that ensnared the country with the blossoming lemons on all sides - as Goethe called Italy, when for once the petals of a local orchid did not obscure his view. Besides Stephanie and me, our crew always consisted of Peter, Florian, Ida and Silvia, all fellow students from Bavaria who were already earning good money as lawyers or judges and could therefore afford extensive vacation. Some of us had also already gained experience with dinghies on the Bavarian lakes and acquired boating licenses, and so we could always charter our own yacht without a skipper. I myself was also the proud owner of a license from the German Sailing Association, which I had acquired while still a student at the end of a two-week trip in Croatia. As there was a hopeless calm at the time of the exam in the early morning, the examiner chose a fictitious wind direction and had the candidates carry out all sailing maneuvers under motor. Hence my now even officially certified knowledge of sailing.

Thus equipped, we went sailing for one or two weeks a year, preferably in the good value early and late seasons of March to June and September to October, when it is far too cold for real Italians at the sea and only Scandinavians and Germans thought to be crazy go swimming. Nevertheless, the weather was usually good, and we grilled ourselves in the sun on deck during the day and fish, freshly bought from the cutter, around the campfire in the evening. If you don't overdo it athletically, which was far from our minds as humanities majors in about our twentieth semester, sailing is a comfortable seaside vacation in a water bungalow that is always with you. Well equipped with kitchen, bathroom and salon, it can be moved from one beautiful bay to the next, to places that are out of reach for package tourists.

There was just one tiny catch: if you charter a yacht once a year as an athletically and technically not particularly skilled contemporary, you sail it with the aplomb of an old lady who, at the wheel of her Mercedes, covers three kilometers to the cemetery twice a year, for which the second gear is of course far enough. Or that of a sports pilot, who is likely to be a dentist in his main profession, who gets lost with his Cessna after a show-off flight over his posh suburb and thus forces a nearby international airport to close.

We have plenty of such glories to come up with. On one of our first trips we blocked the harbor entrance of Cali on Salina for half a day because we ran out of diesel, had to drop anchor and hitchhike to the next petrol station on the island. In the harbor of Capri we stole the show from ageing film stars when our anchor got blocked in a tangle of hawsers from fishing boats. Moored as a major tourist attraction, it took us hours to free it. Another time we sank the anchor of a charter ship, which had been carelessly left unsecured at the end of the chain by the previous crew, in the Korcula harbor basin. The fishermen on the quay then recommended that we hire a local combat diver who is said to have been a notorious sniper in Sarajevo. He actually brought it back up to us without scuba gear from a depth of thirteen meters. Near Olbia we damaged the keel of a brand new charter yacht when we failed to read the chart correctly and ran aground on a rock, all without the extraneous intervention of a siren. Sadly, this was to be imitated years later by a huge cruise ship off the island of Giglio.

As can be assumed, we did not go down in the history of Christian seafaring through these heroic deeds. However, we had the chance to do so during a rescue operation off Elba, where we assisted a bizarre crew of men, for once not from Italy, but from our home country Bavaria, in the greatest distress at sea. We had met the crew beforehand, namely at the base of our charter company in Porto Ferraio - a friendly little town with an impressive fortress watching over the entrance to a wide bay, a wonderful natural harbor. Our sailing companions were eight compatriots who, with their skipper Edmund, known as Edi, had chartered a thirty-nine foot vessel called Andromeda for the same week as us. At the pier we lay alongside them, and the base manager, a Swiss dropout named Giorgio, instructed us after them-expertly and with some disdain for the category of Sunday sailors in general and bookworms in particular-in the use of our vessel. If Andromeda was an Ethiopian king's daughter to be sacrificed to a sea monster, after all, the namesake of our ship was annoying a Greek philosopher. We are talking about Xanthippe.

While we were stocking up on the usual supplies such as drinks, fruit and vegetables, tinned meals, noodles and a large quantity of biscuits for overnight trips, we noticed that our neighbors had brought no less than eight carriers full of local Ichnusa beer and about ten bottles of schnapps. The bulky beer crates could only be stowed on board with difficulty.

"Never mind, they'll be gone soon anyway," Edi commented on the loading process. As is well known, even in the golden age of windjammers, seafaring only worked thanks to many barrels of rum, and so we only joked about the drinking strength of our compatriots, but otherwise attached no importance to the liquid provisions.

The next morning we left the port of Porto Ferraio with the Xanthippe in beautiful sunshine and a light breeze. Under an emphatically democratic ship's command with six captains we only managed a chaotic casting off maneuver, because one of the rear mooring lines got caught on a bollard and the boat turned in the wrong direction. Our Bavarian friends, on the other hand, set sail confidently, each crew member armed with a beer bottle. As a farewell they greeted superior with

"Ahoy". On the mast they set what must have been a self-created flag, showing a black pirate's head on a white and blue background. In its lower right corner roared a lion with a lozenge, similar to the flag of the Bavarian Christian Unity Party. This is what they must have looked like, the lords of the seven Bavarian seas!

To take advantage of the light breeze, we switched off the engine while still in the harbor bay and set mainsail and headsail. Routinely we closed hatches and sea valves and set the radio to the distress channel. The Xanthippe lay diagonally in the water and glided elegantly past the Porto Ferraio fortress rock, putting us landlubbers in high spirits. The Andromeda had extended her initial lead and was now sailing about three hundred yards ahead of us on a course along the island towards Cape Enfola.

Their crew also thought they were in a great mood and sang the well-known old sailor songs *These is a Hofbräuhaus in Munich, Beer here or I'll fall over* and *How drunk they were, the old knightly folk!* After that, what a break in style, *We have to stop drinking less,* a notorious song of German tourists who booze the sangria from tubs on Mallorca.

As we left the cape behind us, I noticed at the helm that we were slowly closing the gap to Andromeda. Not without satisfaction I concluded that our sail trim and my sovereign helm control were superior to the drinking competitors after all. A few minutes later we overtook the Andromeda, whose helmsman Edi had meanwhile exchanged the beer bottle for a rum bottle. Although the Andromeda was also running under full sail, she seemed to be heavier in the water than the Xanthippe. Her loudly singing crew waved over to us as we sailed hard past her on the wind. As we did so, the Andromeda got into the lee, which increased our lead.

After this maneuver we set course for Bastia on Corsica, which we hoped to reach in the evening after seven to nine hours of sailing. The wind freshened so that we had to reef the mainsail in order not to get too much leaning. Thanks to our democratic ship management with the six captains, this maneuver also took a bit of time, but was successful. We had already lost sight and sense of the Andromeda, which had fallen behind us, when suddenly an excited voice on the distress channel disturbed the sailing idyll: "Andromeda calling Xanthippe, urgent! "

"What's up?" asked Peter back from our crew, in defiance of all the radio routines we'd had to cram for the exam.

"We have a water inrush on board, the cabin is flooded, the water is already up to the chart table, and our pump can't make it, get here quick!" shouted Edi from the Andromeda frantically.

"Is this a joke now or what, it's deep here, there are no rocks and no high waves," Peter objected.

"We don't know where the water is coming from either, but it's getting higher, come quickly, please," Edi followed up.

Of course, we then took the call for help seriously. We dropped off course and tacked, switched on the engine as well as the sails and headed for the Andromeda at full throttle. From a distance we could see that the ship was low in the water and the waves were crashing over the deck. At a safe distance we hoisted the sails to be more maneuverable with engine power only and not to ram the Andromeda. When we got within shouting distance, our panicked friends jumped into the water and swam towards us, saving us a dangerous mooring maneuver. Everyone was able to get on board safely via the extended swimming ladder at the stern of our ship.

With open mouths we then watched together the sinking of the abandoned Andromeda. The water was already sloshing over the cabin, and in no time at all the mast and rigging sank until the floods had swallowed the whole ship. The flag with the pirate's head on a white and blue background, the proud emblem of the lords of the Bavarian seas, was the last to sink.

Our friends had not only had a fright, but something else as well. "I need a schnapps now," cried Edi, pointing sadly to the spot in the sea where only a whirlpool pointed to the sunken ship: "All of our stuff is gone, the fish can drink it now."

We motored the whole crew back to the charter base at Porto Ferraio, which we should reach in just under two hours. The weather was still perfect with sunshine and low waves. The base manager Giorgio, already warned by radio, received us pale with horror. The loss of a boat at the beginning of the season hit him hard, because negotiations with the insurance company about a replacement would take longer, he said.

The next morning, Giorgio sent a team of divers to the site of the accident. Using the course data from our navigation system, the Andromeda could be located at a depth of about thirty meters. The first dive revealed the secret of her sinking: the ship was lying undamaged on the seabed, only the hatches, the small windows at the bottom of the cabin, were open. That was why water had entered when the ship heeled over on its side after setting sail. And the crew, in their drunken state, didn't notice the boat filling up until it was too late. Edi & Co were in for a hefty bill, as the owner's insurance company would classify their behavior as gross negligence and take recourse against them. The charter company thought it too costly to raise the Andromeda again, and so she remained in her watery grave on the seabed off Elba.

We are still waiting in vain for an award as a sea rescuer. However, the success story of the Bavarian piracy sailing under the flag of the Christian Unity Party got a kink by the sinking of the Andromeda. According to reports, the party itself has not engaged in piracy on the water since then, but has retreated with it into the Bavarian countryside again.

VIII. Pompei on the Costa Smeralda

Wilst in the previous years we had headed out to Elba, the Gulf of Naples and the Aeolian Islands off Sicily, we decided this year to charter a yacht on Sardinia, more precisely in the northeast of the island near the port city of Olbia. With us were again Stephanie, Peter, Florian, Ida and Silvia. We were attracted by the archipelago of La Maddalena and the Costa Smeralda (Emerald Coast) with its turquoise water like in the Caribbean. This stretch of land was bought up by a certain Mr Aga Khan, an Arab sheik or something like that, from shepherds in the fifties in order to build exclusive holiday resorts for celebrities around the retort Porto Cervo - which sounds decidedly better than the translation *deer harbor*.

In this area, further south in the Gulf of Marinella, lay another treat: the estate of a well-known politician, bon vivant and colorful personality, whom the attentive reader has already encountered in other stories. On a modest forty hectares of land, the same size as his harmless counterpart in the Vatican, the Croesus dubbed Cavaliere (Knight) had had a villa ensemble built with a moderate size of 2,600 square meters of living space. According to the gossip columns, the property also contained an artificially created lake, seven swimming pools, a greenhouse with orchids, palms and numerous species of cacti from all over the world, centuries-old olive trees, an amphitheater and, just to round things off, some artificial waterfalls.

Unfortunately, unscrupulous envious people, presumably from the ranks of the communists, brought the property into disrepute in public, and this only because of a few modest parties. Of these, a Sardinian paparazzo took several hundred photos from a safe distance with a telephoto lens, which Silvio claimed were completely harmless. After being banned from circulation by the courts in Italy, the Spanish newspaper *El Pais* printed them. They showed nothing more interesting than the badly worn private parts of some equally worn politicians and an armada of scantily or even less clad society ladies.

To Silvio's credit, it should be noted that although all the ladies were flown in at state expense, demonstrably only one of them, namely the Minister for Posts, Telecommunications and New Media, was also a member of the government. It is undoubtedly an emancipatory approach beyond criticism to fob off secondary ladies of the heart not only with castles, palaces, precious stones, flowers, cigarette cases or, as in Bavaria, with scented soaps, but also to provide them with professional prospects in the government of a country. To journalists, Silvio once boasted, "I'm just doing what all men would like to do. "He then blandly tried to talk his way out of it, because last night he had had to give up shamefully early, namely already with the eighth of the eleven ladies he had ordered, for fitness reasons. Although he was only in his early seventies at the time!

The property also made headlines for a system of secret passages and grottos with Roman statues and mosaics, betrayed by spies among the guests, which was modelled on early James Bond films. This was supposed to provide a link between the villas and the nearby sea. In addition, the ridiculous accusation of some left-wing journalists was that the whole thing had been built in disregard of all legal regulations in a nature and water conservation area, after bribing the local authorities.

Confidently, Silvio countered that nothing less than the existential security interests of the country required the secrecy of the structure. For in case of defense, only the hidden passages allowed him to reach the sea from the villas, to be picked up there by a submarine, and to organize the national defense as commander-in-chief of the armed forces. There would have been no need for these objections, however, since the Sardinian authorities did not bring proceedings against King Silvio anyway, who spread his benefactions over the island. Instead, they heeded the old saying: *He who pays the piper calls the tune.*

Inspired by these reports, we chugged to the Gulf of Marinella on the second day of our trip, hoping to spot something of Silvio's parties with binoculars. The press had just reported his return to Sardinia. Unfortunately we were not alone with this idea, because in the gulf loitered about some twenty yachts from different countries. The entrance to the bay was blocked by a patrol boat of the nature protection authority, which had to supervise the anchor prohibition valid there and the minimum distance of 200 meters to the coast. It was treacherous that these rules were so strictly controlled here. The impression was that in addition to the natural beauty, the local fauna - namely lushly developed female mammals during the mating season - should also be protected.

Because of the patrol boat we left disappointed. Except for a few garden walls and tall trees, nothing could be seen from a distance, neither with the telephoto lens nor the binoculars. Since the day was already advanced, we decided to spend the night in a nearby bay outside the restricted area. Once there, we dug the anchor into the sandy seabed in textbook fashion with the engine in reverse. After that we went ashore with the dinghy, in which we loaded all the barbecue utensils. In the morning we had been able to buy a cat shark from a fisherman, who offered it to us as a tasty barbecue fish. On the beach we started a campfire with pieces of driftwood and coal, bordered by two quickly built stone walls. On these we put the grill grate, which we had found in a box on board.

Grilled cat shark with garlic bread on raw fennel and chocolate biscuits for dessert is a little-known menu, and quite rightly so, as it turned out. The shark turned out tough and tasted less like fish than like a boiling chicken mistaken for a rooster and accidentally landed on the grill. Driven by hunger, we nevertheless ate everything.

We were just about to drown the frustration about the luckless photo safari and the modest dinner in gallons of Sardinian country wine and to slip into a pleasant pre-sleep, when Peter started up as if stung by a tarantula: On a slope not far from us, in the direction of the Gulf of Marinella, a red fire roller was building up, illuminating the bay more and more brightly.

"Does anyone have any idea what that is? ", Peter asked startled in the round.

"It's going to be a huge fire and it's coming right at us, ouch, I can feel the heat already too," Silvia cried out beside herself.

"If this is a volcanic eruption, like the one at Vesuvius," exclaimed Florian, who had visited Pompei before the sailing holiday, "then that's it now, we can forget about us."

"But I've never heard of any active volcano in Sardinia," I interjected.

"You never know, there are also dormant volcanoes that take millennia to awaken," Florian countered expertly.

Fittingly, I remembered what I had learned when preparing a presentation on volcanoes for a geography class at school: First there is an eruption of ash, lava and gases, accompanied by a rain of pumice and an earthquake. Then the volcano spews out huge amounts of magma, which combines with the lava to form downhill mega-flows that bury everything underneath. If a person has survived it all this far, they now die in a pyroclastic storm, a blaze of gases and molten rock up to 800 degrees that wipes out all life, even on ships in port. Even farther away, one can perish from pyroclastic flows and sulfuric fumes, as Pliny the Elder did back close to Stabiae..."

Suddenly Ida's roar interrupted my flow of thoughts, "There's a rumble really loud, it might be an earthquake."

We were gripped by naked fear. The wall of fire now took on huge dimensions and lit up the bay as bright as day. And suddenly the earth began to tremble as well.

"I just wanted to have a normal holiday with you," Ida sobbed, facing Florian, "because I had to fall in love with that idiot with his volcano stories... and now we're all going to die, my mum will never forgive me for that... I should have stayed with Manfred, in hillbilly Lower Bavaria, there I would have seen a volcano on TV at most... but now it's happened, what a pity, I still had a lot planned in life..."

We froze in shock, images of our previous lives flashed before us, and we mentally prepared ourselves for the lava flow under which we were to evaporate in a split second.

But contrary to all fears, nothing happened, and after a few minutes we were still sitting silently around the campfire, waiting for our approaching end. But at some point I noticed that the wall of fire was getting smaller and sirens were wailing somewhere.

Gradually we regained our composure and in our minds returned to life. The sirens became louder.

"There's a fire brigade moving out somewhere, so maybe it was just an ordinary fire or something," Peter speculated.

Only now did it occur to us to return on board as quickly as possible so that we could escape with the ship if necessary. Without packing up our things, we pushed the dinghy into the water and rowed back to the yacht at full speed. Unimpressed by the impending end of the world, it still lay calmly at anchor.

By the time we got back on deck via the swim ladder, the wall of fire over the Gulf of Marinella was almost extinguished.

"It's getting smaller now, we got away with it again," Peter placated. "But let's turn on the radio, maybe we'll find out something. "

So we did, and didn't have to wait long on *Rai Uno*'s radio program: "And here's a message for the residents of Porto Rotondo and the surrounding area in Sardinia. Recently a wall of fire and a supposed earthquake caused fear and confusion among the population. According to an urgent message of the fire brigade Olbia it is not a natural disaster, but an artificial volcanic eruption on the estate of the Prime Minister Silvio Berlusconi in the gulf of Marinella. This was not announced and was apparently staged for the entertainment of the party guests. There is no danger whatsoever, and it is strongly advised to remain calm..."

And so we have still got some live experience from the Sardinian estate of Silvio. You should not underestimate him, this volcano of a man!

IX. Rough customs in South Tyrol

South Tyrol is a remote corner at the end of the Italian world, where human civilization recoils from rocky massifs, impassable gorges and wild rivers. If in the northern Alps mountains and valleys are arranged in a reasonably symmetrical and disciplined manner, in South Tyrol and the adjacent Trentino there is a fabulous confusion. The Dolomites flaunt rebellious jags, anarchic figures, defiant turrets and oriels, deep cuts and lush curves in all the wrong places. Mountains and valleys are interspersed with forested belts of hills, gentle plateaus and lakes gleaming in unashamed blue. Apparently, the good Lord didn't lay out this landscape during standard working time, but cobbled it together after hours over an aperitif at a bar, distracted by a snow fairy with a beaming smile and a glass of Bombardino in hand. In short, the Dolomites provide a taste of the even greater chaos further south, in the Italian heartlands.

On the other hand, the people of South Tyrol are still in order. Untouched by the temptations of the licentious life, they eke out a meagre existence in old wooden houses. They earn their daily bread with hard work. In summer they drive the cattle up to the alpine pastures and cut the forage grass out of steep mountain slopes with a scythe. In autumn they harvest grapes and press delicious wine that delights the senses and the soul. And in winter they work with sledges in the forest and sit by the crackling stove fire in the evening, carving nativity figures, tying brooms and repairing shoes and clothes. On Sundays they march in their colorful traditional costumes to the church above the village and praise God in song and prayer, in German of course. Unfortunately, the Austrians lost

South Tyrol to Italy after the First World War, and with respect to their loyal friend Mussolini, the Nazis also accepted this. Apart from this unfortunate coincidence, the world there is still intact.

At least that's what trendy advertising brochures, leisure magazines and websites try to convince the six million or so German tourists every year. They invade the idyllic paradise with their premium vehicles, off-road motorcycles and private planes. They head to mega-ski resorts, with hundreds of lifts and thousands of kilometers of pistes connecting ever more valleys. Or they visit almost as cool cross-country ski centers and *all-year fitness* and *wellness temples*. Still others indulge in the new-fangled sports of *heliskiing, river rafting, canyoning* and *bungee jumping.* And in the evening they settle down in rustic hotel parlors made of pine wood to enjoy the seven-course pampering menu with drinks included in the package price.

The scenically no less beautiful Alpine regions in Veneto and Friuli, which only attract a few hundred thousand tourists a year, are therefore green with envy. Nevertheless, they have not yet decided to introduce Teutonic as an official language. After all, in the meantime they too are luring tourists with attractions such as *bivouacs for gourmets, wholesome mountain forests, blossoming climbing gardens, freshly cooled torrents and fermenting lakes* in German-language glossy brochures.

Or with *holiday homes with polished individual toilets, bathing sluts for all and children free*. Even Thai tourism could take a leaf out of this book. By the way, the translation, generously financed by a European regional fund, was done by the son of the local tourism director, who is learning German as a second foreign language in his third year at high school.

Although we only wanted to do old-fashioned mountain hiking, we were also drawn to the South Tyrolean paradise, as it is so conveniently located between Bavaria and Tuscany. And so, on a beautiful September afternoon at around half past three o'clock, I found myself with my student friend Peter on the ascent to the Edelweiß lodge in the Pflersch valley. This flows only a short distance from the Brenner Pass into the main valley through which the Eisack river flows. We wanted to do a multi-day hike on high-altitude trails with magnificent views that are too strenuous for the majority of tourists. At least that's what our hiking guide boasted in his perfidious way of singling out its buyers from the tourist masses as the chosen few.

On the hiking map, the climb from the parking lot to the lodge didn't look close, and there were also about a thousand meters of altitude to climb. But the information given by the landlord on the phone with a rustic South Tyrolean accent: "one and a half hours on foot, comfortable" took away all our worries. With courageous steps and not so light backpacks we started the ascent, which was on a gravel road for the first time. The lodge could also have been reached on this road, but we soon turned off onto the steeper mountain path recommended by the hiking guide.

Slowly the forest thinned out and the path revealed ever more magnificent views of the valley and the surrounding mountain ranges with their jagged peaks. After an hour, we were already quite exhausted because of our brisk pace and took a rest on the bench in front of a small chapel. An inscription above the entrance door said that the valley inhabitants had built it several hundred years ago as a place to rest for pilgrims. After a proper snack of sandwiches, I took a look at the map, where I didn't find the chapel at first. Then I spotted a black cross at the edge of the dotted trail line, not so far from the parking lot.

"This can't be the chapel, we must have walked further," I said to Peter.

"Let's see, maybe we did not, and the fellow told us nonsense," he countered brightly.

In fact, the landlord had not told us the truth. The path initially flattened out again, but this was followed by an intermediate climb. Over this we reached a small high valley, which narrowed in places to a gorge. In the middle of it, a stream with majestic waterfalls roared, pouring into bubbling pools. The path along the water was exposed in places, but very beautiful. A few wind-blown pines stood on the narrow bank, but mighty cliffs rose just behind them. But even after two hours there was no sign of the lodge. We now paid the price for having underestimated the distance and started off at too high a speed. Completely exhausted, we only longed for our arrival at the lodge.

But the next thing we knew, there were snowfields ahead of us that had to be crossed. In these shady areas at over 2,000 meters, the snow lasted well into the summer months. Every step was arduous, we often sank in knee-deep and only made progress at a snail's pace. After a while, the trail left the stream valley to wind its way up a mountainside on steep gravel fields. Once at the top, we had been walking for three hours now, we suddenly saw the lodge standing on the next hill. It was perched on a yoke lined with huge boulders that held two snow-covered peaks together like a ribbon.

The closeness to the finish spurred us, and so we took the final climb again more spiritedly. Slowly the day was running out, it was already dusk. The setting sun illuminated the mountain massifs, shrouding them in mild veils of light, and a fairy landscape took hold with its shadows. Soon the sun had completely disappeared and the peaks shone in a pale red - the legendary alpenglow! A natural spectacle that compensated us for the exertions of the ascent. Quite incongruously, Sigi Sommer's *cinema heroes* came to mind: *The villain lies prostrate in the dust, and through his chest riddled with bullets, one sees the last rays of the setting evening sun.*

At seven o'clock we finally stood in front of the lodge, it had taken us no less than three and a half hours. From the outside it made an inconspicuous impression, with roughly plastered stone walls that would have needed a new coat of paint. Inside, the parlor shone freshly renovated in what is called the Bavarian yodeling style, with solid wooden benches and tables in front of paneled walls, decorated with a surrounding frieze of carvings. These depicted scenes of country life: lively maids and farmhands harvesting hay, mountain dwellers mowing scythes on a steep slope, and a tractor with trailer in front of a farmhouse with wooden shutters decorated with blooming flowers in pots, at the point of being refueled.

"Hello, I'm Robert. Are you the two Germans who have registered for this afternoon, you are quite late! ", a corpulent gentleman with a reddish swollen skull greeted us.

"Yes, it took us much longer than we thought, not an hour and a half as you said, but three and a half. "

"My darlings, of course I can't help it if you two are such flatland Tyroleans and approach the climb like a city stroll. You're just not here in the Munich pedestrian zone on the way to eating sausages in a restaurant!"

This much was already only too clear to us. Offended in our honor, we protested: "Yes, but who can manage a thousand meters of altitude in one and a half hours?

"Yes, you can, if you are well on your feet; perhaps you have not found the path on the right, where you can take a short cut," returned Robert. We had seen nothing of such a path, nor did the map show it. "But now you are here, and arriving is everything, otherwise nothing counts. I'll offer you a fruit schnapps as a welcome drink," he concluded.

As attested by his pancake face and handsome graveyard of dumplings, which extended downward into a traffic jam on the ring road (as the Bavarians call it), Robert possessed a high level of liquor expertise, which he must have acquired through decades of practice. Surely he'd driven himself up in a jeep, no way an hour and a half's comfortable walk! Then out of the kitchen door stepped a skinny, maybe eighteen-year-old boy with a tray and three shot glasses on it, who introduced himself as Valentin. I guess he was some kind of apprentice and did the real work around here.

The welcome schnapps apparently represented a ritual practiced with all guests. Robert routinely emptied his glass in one go, wished us a pleasant stay and referred us to Valentin for the room handover and "everything administrative". He then came to our table with the lodge book, we entered our names, and as a spontaneous revenge we wrote in the column profession *lodge inspectors of the German Alpine Club,* but Valentin didn't pay any attention. We were assigned a room with two beds, toilet and shower in the corridor.

"Think nothing of it," added Valentine; "Robert drinks a little too much since his wife ran away a few years ago, and he has had to manage the lodge lone, but otherwise he is harmless!"

We nodded in understanding. Terribly famished, we wanted to place a small food order with Valentin right away. We were thinking of trout carpaccio to set the mood, then saddle of venison with cranberries and dumplings and red cabbage as the main course, and finally a Tyrolean apple strudel in vanilla sauce, or instead a Sacher cake with cream?, when two pretty Italian women of our age staggered through the door of the lodge. In their sneakers, short pants and sweaty shirts, they looked completely exhausted, as if they were about to collapse.

"Where's the lodge-keeper here?" they gasped. "How can he tell us that it takes an hour to get up there, and we've been walking for four hours now, and we didn't have enough water and food with us?"

"Don't get so worked up, it's bad for your beauty," Robert groaned in broken Italian and immediately added: "You're not properly equipped for a mountain tour with your sneakers. You might be able to go to a tennis court in Milan or to a disco in Bolzano to dance, but you can't go hiking in the high mountains. Take these two young men from Bavaria as an example," Robert pointed at us, "it only took them an hour to get up there."

That did it, that really was enough! Apparently he thought we didn't understand. I now explained to the two hiking princesses in Italian: "Don't be fooled, this is a huge nonsense, he also told us that the climb to the lodge only takes one and a half hours, but then we needed over three hours and are now just as exhausted as you are".

Robert apparently appreciated this clarification less and turned away without a word. "What a jerk," the smaller, petite princess called after him, and then introduced herself as "Mara, pleased to meet you." So we were able to start forming delicate bonds with the two beauties right away. Mara and Marina, the name of the other, slightly stockier princess, looked athletic but had never been to the Alps before. After a major exam in their design studies at the University of Bologna, they wanted to try mountain hiking. But this first attempt was a complete failure.

After some small talk about studies and universities, we suggested a game in which everyone gets a piece of paper with the name of a person known to all participants pinned to their forehead, which they then have to guess. While the two princesses gave us the names Leonardo da Vinci and Benito Mussolini, we slyly attached their own names to them to learn more about them.

Mara immediately started with the question "Am I an actress and mistress of James Bond?", but I had to excuse myself for a visit to the throne room. The way led past the open kitchen door, and there I stopped, electrified, and could not believe my ears: "Have you seen these two jerks, they're writing me straight into the lodge book *Inspectors of the German Alpine Club*. That would be the first time these bastards from Munich send me someone to inspect, don't you think? But I won't let myself be fooled by such weirdos, they must be from some university and their parents spoil them like hell, I don't believe them," Robert raged.

"You also deceived everyone with the ascent time of one and a half hours, whereas we ourselves need two and a half, and then also the scam with your climb on the right, which doesn't even exist anymore!" shot back Valentin.

"I guess we're allowed to have a little fun, if we're already busting our asses day in and day out for these strangers!", Robert defended himself and added: "And now they're making out with these two Italian chicks, acting like they want to play some stupid game, but they just want to get them laid, it's obvious," Robert continued to hiss.

"If I didn't have to hold back with the guests, I'd try that too," Valentin admitted disarmingly.

"You know what, I'll tell the women right now that those two jerks will be flat after the climb anyway and won't be able to," Robert reasoned.

"You can't bring that up, they are guests here after all, and maybe they really are inspectors," Valentin countered.

My goodness, these are rough customs here in South Tyrol, I thought and sidled away silently in the direction of the toilet so as not to be discovered.

"Am I a wanted criminal, a robbery killer who dismembers her victims?" asked Marina as I returned to the game, but at that moment the door opened and a group of Italian men strutted in. All of them looked dressed up as if they were on their way to a business dinner, wearing black suits, expensive leather shoes, and gold chains around their necks, something along the lines of car salesmen, insurance salesmen, marriage con artists, or county chairmen of the neo-fascist party. They must have driven up in a jeep, after a few hours of hiking you wouldn't look so good, I guessed.

"Good evening, can we stay here for dinner?" they called out towards the counter and immediately took a seat at an adjacent table as well.

Robert turned quietly to Valentin: "I don't need any more of those Italian showboats from the city. They have no business in a mountain lodge, you don't drive up there in a jeep dressed like a show-off, we're not a specialty restaurant for snobs!"

"Am I Pope Benedict the Sixteenth?" asked Peter, and one of the men with a well-groomed moustache, probably the head of the personal liability and household inventory insurance department, demanded the menu. Robert nodded and placed an ornate card on the table for the new guests, openly displaying his displeasure with them.

"Do you also have an Italian card? Everything in there is only in German," the head of department requested.

"No," Robert replied pointedly, adding in bad Italian, "You're here in a mountain lodge in the Tyrol, we speak German here."

"No, we're in Italy here," the head of the department corrected him indignantly, "and there has to be an Italian menu, that would be a scandal otherwise."

"We don't have anything else, kiss my ass and cook for yourself," Robert snorted and turned away from the table of men demonstratively again.

"We want the Italian menu immediately or we'll call the police, you can't be discriminated against as a foreigner in your own country," the head of department clamored.

"You're welcome to try that," Robert returned victoriously, "we'll see if it does you any good then."

The police would hardly drive up to a mountain lodge in the evening, I thought, but in the meantime I had recognized my name and wanted to savor the whole thing a little more: "Is there a painting of mine of a woman with a magical look hanging in the Louvre? And did I have two of my students fall to their deaths with a self-made flying machine?" as it says on a memorial plaque on a lookout point near Fiesole.

"Am I an Italian who had many German friends? ", Peter also approached his puzzle hero.

"Yes, you could put it that way, but then the Italians eventually resented you," Mara countered.

Now Valentin came with the food and we interrupted the game. First he served our trout carpaccio and a barley soup with vegetables and mushrooms for the princesses. This was still reasonably balanced. Driven by hunger, we devoured the appetizer without really enjoying the noble fish fillet. The princesses also spooned away their delicious looking oat soup in no time. Then followed for us gigantic portions of saddle of venison with dumplings and cranberry sauce, plus blue cabbage, served stylishly in their own bowls.

The huge pieces of meat made me wonder, maybe it was a deer, a wild boar or even an eloped bear that had to bite the dust. Our counterparts were satisfied with an *insalata caprese,* tomatoes with mozzarella and basil. The caloric imbalance was now hard to deny. The princesses gave us disturbed looks over the mounds of meat and, to make matters worse, outed themselves as vegetarians. Perhaps we did not fully satisfy their demands in terms of food culture and sustainable nutrition. Even more embarrassing was the dessert, because in order to somehow avoid the agony of choosing between apple strudel and Sachertorte, we had simply ordered both for everyone. Fortunately the princesses let themselves be invited to two desserts, and so the mood was saved. After dinner, we then resumed our game, but were brusquely interrupted.

"Who called us here? ", the policemen, whom I had not heard coming, snapped at the guests of the lodge.

"It was us," the head of the insurance department explained, "as we've already told you by phone, we're being deliberately discriminated against here; the landlord pretends not to understand us, and withholds the Italian menu from us."

"What do you think, Robert? ," the older of the policemen now asked in German.

"I can't explain it at all, I'm sure there's an Italian menu on that table too, we really have quite a few of those," Robert squirmed. Then, with a suspicious hand movement worthy of a pickpocket, he fished something from the men's table and handed it to the policemen.

"There it is, the Italian menu! ", laughed the older policeman, "today's special is roast wild boar in red wine sauce with ribbon noodles and chanterelles and doughnuts for dessert, that sounds quite tasty, doesn't it?"

"I can’t believe it!," howled one of the men, "all this time we've been asking for it, and the landlord kept repeating he didn't have an Italian menu. We swear!"

"You know what, dear friend," the older policeman snapped at the Italians, "if you're going to make us come up this mountain again for nothing, you might as well come with us. We've got a couple of nice cells left at the station, freshly painted, I'm sure you'd feel right at home there in your snazzy suits."

The Italians froze, pale and unable to utter another word. "Good night, Robert, don't worry," the policemen bid farewell. Shortly afterwards, the Italians, led by the head of the private liability insurance department, dejectedly left the room. Outside, you could still hear engines starting up and cars driving away, then it was quiet again.

"Salvini or Mussolini, who am I now?, "Peter asked triumphantly, and Robert turned to us with a wink: "I only did that for you so that you wouldn't be disturbed tonight with your new friends. I hope you'll put that in the report for the German Alpine Club!"

X. In the footsteps of Lully

During the semesters that we spent at the institute on research work and seminars, I also indulged in the hobby of music. In this context, only uninitiated laymen will express the opinion that playing orchestra music is less dangerous than hiking in the mountains or sailing. In reality, it is precisely the handling of musical instruments and equipment that harbors unimagined risks to human health.

This is testified to by the tragic fate of the famous Florentine musician Giovanni Battista Lulli. Born in 1632 as the musically gifted son of a poor family, he arrived in Paris in his childhood as - as an older encyclopedia calls it - the page of a rich noblewoman. There he became friends with the later Sun King Louis XIV at the court in his youth. Under the name Jean-Baptiste Lully he had an unprecedented career as composer, musician and dancer, which even brought him the elevation to the nobility. His decline began in the 1680s, when a new mistress of the king drove him from court because she disapproved of his lavish homosexuality. Yet Lully courted reconciliation with his childhood friend, the king, at every opportunity. This came about in 1686, after the king had almost perished - and not even gloriously in war, but at the hands of his dentists. While pulling a tooth, they tore out a piece of his upper jaw, and the bleeding wound had to be cauterized with a red-hot iron. The whole court expected the king to die, but he recovered. For the celebrations of his recovery, Lully prepared a great composition: an enormous Te Deum with the court chapel, which consisted of no less than three hundred musicians. But during a performance at the Église des Pères Feuillants in Paris in early 1687, a fatal accident occurred: as was customary at the time, Lully beat the rhythm on the floor with a heavy conducting stick, clumsily hitting a toe. The injury became inflamed and infected with gangrene, from which the musician died a few months later.

I was to encounter such musical dangers myself in Italy, but I have to backtrack a bit. Many years earlier, while still a Bavarian high school student, I had pursued a musical career for a time. I took lessons in piano and violin and dreamed of a life as an orchestral musician. Several talented members of our school orchestra, who later made the leap to professional musician and now play in well-known orchestras, spurred me on. On their advice, I switched from the violin to the more cumbersome viola, which plays only a service role in most pieces. My role models said that this instrument was necessary in every orchestra, but less desirable. Admittedly, I had to discover that violists, who were considered rather reprieved than gifted, often became the laughing stock of the entire orchestra, similar to the East Frisians in Germany. With the only difference being that it was justified with the violists (such as: A Santa Claus, an Easter Bunny, a good and a bad violist are waiting at a traffic light. Who will cross the street first? Answer: The bad violist, because the others don't exist).

When I failed the entrance examination to the conservatory at the end of my schooling, I continued my musical career for a while in old people's homes in the immediate vicinity and as a substitute organist in the branch churches of my home parish, until my law studies put an abrupt end to it. From then on I only played in student orchestras for pleasure. Even after my arrival in Florence, I looked around for a lay orchestra, although there are far fewer of them in Italy than in Germany. I also hoped that I might meet more nice Italians in an orchestra. I then learned that, although not the Institute, the State University of Florence had recently opened an orchestra. I got in touch with them and, as a sought-after violist, they invited me to the next rehearsal.

On my first evening there, I met many amazing characters, but few Italian students. The conductor was the likeable Marco, a short and, by Italian standards, unusually blond violin teacher from Puglia. He knew how to conduct discreetly and precisely. The first violin was played by Beatrice, a petite Italian who studied violin at the conservatory and was actually far too good for the orchestra. Less lofty writers would claim of her that she was only after the married Marco, but of course I do not wish to engage in such vulgar speculation. Several other orchestra musicians were sympathetic German and Austrian exchange students who had also fallen for the strategic illusion that they could meet like-minded Italians in the orchestra. The first cello was played by Virginie, a slightly crazy French student with delicate features who always showed up for rehearsals in baroque dress. Without envy, I have to admit that her French accent sounded a bit more graceful in Italian than my Bavarian one.

In addition, the orchestra included adults from all over the world who had ended up in Florence after colorful journeys through life. There was an oddball and notoriously badly shaven Calabrese with black horn-rimmed glasses named Vito, who also played the viola. Instead of a greeting, he immediately asked me at the first rehearsal if I also felt so much fear in cemeteries because there were so many crosses there (in reality, he meant sharps). Years ago Vito had followed a blonde from the south of Sweden, who towered over him by a head, to her hometown of Hamburg and had learned a decent amount of German there. But at some point she didn't like his nose and its immediate surroundings so much any longer. After all, the years in Germany helped him to get a job as an occasional interpreter for the municipal police after his return to Italy. Thanks to the almost solidary petty crime of his Calabrian compatriots against tourists in Florence, he was able to keep his head above water.

I was also impressed by the American painter couple Richard and Anne Maury, who played the violin and cello respectively. Stephanie and I soon became friends with them, and they often invited us to dine and play quartets in their apartment in a former convent on the Costa San Giorgio, from which one has a wonderful view over the old town. Both were already in their early sixties and had emigrated to Florence from the United States decades ago to live in what they said was an artistically inspiring environment. Richard pursued a radically realistic style in painting that made his pictures look almost like photographs, only somehow more concise and impressive (you can admire a selection of them on the Internet). Anne painted mainly flowers and bushes for art prints, plant books and cards. After a dry spell of many years, Richard had his breakthrough in the 1980s when, with the help of a New York gallerist, he was able to gain a foothold in the American market.

A friendly atmosphere soon arose in this motley ensemble. Our first performance took place at the end of the semester in the festival hall of the university on the Piazza San Marco. There we provided the musical accompaniment for the awarding of certificates, as they say. The program included movements from an early Mozart symphony, Beethoven's Coriolan Overture, and some dances and arias in the old style by Ottorino Respighi, a pleasing Italian version of impressionism. The performance apparently impressed the president of the university, who presided over the ceremony. For at the reception afterwards he kept ruminating that he couldn't believe that the university now had such a great ensemble, that we had sprung up like a happy musical mushroom, and that in any case he now wanted to make something of us.

What this meant in concrete terms we were to find out at the next rehearsal two weeks later. Marco sadly informed us that in the future he would play first violin next to Beatrice, he had been replaced as conductor of the orchestra. As a new conductor we got a professional from the Fiesolan Conservatory of Music, who had already conducted the Italian National Youth Orchestra: Nicola Razskevski, a brawny thoroughbred musician who exuded more Prussian austerity than Italian charm. With him, the atmosphere was no longer as cordial as under Marco, for he demanded respect and always had the individual voices audition separately. In this way he mercilessly exposed you if you hadn't practiced properly.

After such an audition of the five violas, which ended atonally in five voices, contrary to the composer's intention, Vito again advised with the helpful insight that we must now procure better instruments, which had already been played in higher positions. But all in all the orchestra improved visibly. Under Nicola we now also rehearsed more modern pieces such as the First

Symphony by the great Russian Dimitri Shostakovich, the tragic sound of which our new conductor recreated with unbridled energy. After a few internal auditions, in which even the violas cut a happier figure, the score was in place and we could confidently look forward to the planned performances. Florence, Fiesole, even Bologna were planned - but first Viareggio, a harbor town next to Pisa in the Arnodelta, famous for its carnival.

On a Saturday afternoon in April we drove the eighty kilometers there with two buses chartered by the university. One bus would have been enough for the orchestra, but the university had advertised the concert and offered interested students a free ride. This strategy had perhaps been copied from the German provincial orchestras guesting in Florence, who brought their audience, consisting of retired music lovers from their own booster club, with them in buses. So nothing stood in the way of a triumphant reception in famous halls such as Florence's Teatro della Pergola.

Our concert took place in the Municipal Theatre of Viareggio on the occasion of the commemoration day of the local saint, a typical opportunity for Italian festivities. The orchestra, the ladies in their luxurious evening gowns and the gentlemen in their elegant suits, now also appeared outwardly like a homogeneous body of sound. Nicola appeared all in black, and under his suit he wore not a tie or bow tie, but a neat turtleneck sweater. Before the concert began at six o'clock in the evening, the theatre, a classicistic hall with dark red walls and golden chandeliers, filled up only sluggishly. So the student audience we had brought along from Florence proved useful. Shortly before six, however, the mayor arrived with a large number of faithful, probably city councilors and other big-headed people, who in turn brought along an equally impressive entourage. In the end, the hall was filled to capacity.

No sooner had we taken the stage than we received a round of polite applause, and Nicola gave the start to the first work, Handel's Fireworks Music. This had been commissioned by the English king in 1748 to celebrate the conclusion of peace in the Austrian Succession War. After having thousands and thousands of soldiers slaughter each other, kings and princes have always liked to make peace in solemn ceremonies when war became too costly or no longer fun for them. We managed the piece, which was once again less challenging for violas, flawlessly. Afterwards we played Beethoven's Coriolan Overture again, which was already part of the standard repertoire. The climax before the interval was to be Shostakovich's First Symphony, the sounds of which drift beguilingly back and forth between Romanticism and Modernism.

Already in the opening movement our conductor outdid himself. With his pointed baton, Nicola wheeled around in the air like a possessed sorcerer battling phantoms, and suddenly it happened: in preparation for a majestic intermediate chord, he brought his hands together in a sweeping manner, and in doing so, the baton must have become unhappily entangled, because he rammed it into his left palm with force. Nicola gave an unmistakable cry of pain, and a thin stream of blood shot from his hand. Although Nicola tried to press on the wound with his other hand to stop the flow of blood and shouted "keep going", the orchestra stopped playing in shock. At that moment Virginie, our delicate cellist, slumped; she had fainted, and her cello fell to the floor beside her with a gruff roar.

The mayor already rose from the front row and announced that the concert would unfortunately have to be interrupted because of this accident. That is what happened. Nicola, who had kept himself under control all the time despite the pain, was soon picked up by an ambulance. At the local hospital, the doctors were able to stop his bleeding quickly and put a pressure bandage on it. Everything went smoothly for Virginie too: she soon regained consciousness and was only taken to hospital for a check-up. There it was confirmed that she had sustained no injuries apart from a few minor scrapes to her head. An hour later, Nicola and Virginie returned from the hospital and we took the bus home in a depressed mood.

On the drive, Nicola told us: "You know, the only consolation is that my unspeakably embarrassing mishap has happened to greater musicians before me... There was a Florentine composer at the court of Louis the Fourteenth in Versailles a few hundred years ago. At a festive service in honor of his king, he jammed the baton not into his hand, but into his foot, and then died of blood poisoning..."

"Whereupon he went straight to hell on the baton along with Shostakovich," Vito continued grimly, scolding, "Nicola, you've given us a huge scare today, and that's why you really don't need to tell us fairy tales now!"

XI. A nanny from the First World or wisdom from the white mill

In disrespectful disregard of the former president of the institute's rebuke that more babies were born here than doctoral theses, Stephanie and I had become parents of two girls long before we had completed our work. At least we managed to get married before the birth of our first daughter, to the delight of our not-so-revolutionary families. After that, however, we had to get on with our work straight away, and so we hired a nanny to look after our offspring for a few hours a week.

First we had the trusty Floranna, who had come to Florence from Basilicata in southern Italy to study linguistics. She taught our girls their first Italian. When she went back home after graduation, the whole family mourned her loss. Without question, we needed a replacement. That's why we put an ad in a local rag, to which a real Florentine named Piera unexpectedly responded. At her interview she turned out to be a southern beauty who had parked herself at the university for eight years in psychology, but in real life did all sorts of things - like Indian and Arabic dancing, yoga training and the close supervision of two mongrel dogs and a fellow student whose family had immigrated from Argentina.

As a welcome gift, she brought a bag of *Mulino Bianco* (White Mill) *Ritornelli* (sweeping verses) biscuits, with an advertising slogan printed on the wrapper: "*Seeing you return will certainly be even nicer, thought the cocoa, and bowed his head in greeting to the almond*. And so it was. With her sensitive nature Piera immediately won us over and we engaged her on the spot. We were a little surprised when she drove up in her own car, which is untypical for Italian students. But on closer inspection, it turned out to be an old rust bucket, so we didn't suspect anything.

From then on Piera came three times a week and treated our girls very lovingly. She made games and creative handicrafts with them, and with her they made great progress in Italian. Piera's nice habit of bringing cookies with her continued in the future. This is how we got to know the *Campagnole* (country girls): *she has grown up, but she carries the lush cornfields of her childhood in her heart.*

To read Little Red Riding Hood, Piera brought a bag of *macine* (grindstones), even if their motto was more reminiscent of a hippopotamus than a wolf in drag: *He took one last look at the sea of milk below and dived in.* And a common dinner was sweetened by the *Pan di Stelle* (Star Bread): *If the evening is too dark, spark lights of abundance with the cocoa of the star buns!*

Soon we also met Piera's lovely boyfriend Alessandro, and over tea at her house, at which she served *abbracci* (hugs), we made friends with her naughty but kind-hearted mongrel dogs. They had mottled brown and white coats: *no one ever knew if it was the cocoa that first hugged the cream, or vice versa.* Because of them, she lived in the country and had to commute many miles to the city every day. She only kept her parents a secret - we only learned that they were divorced, but that Piera had a good relationship with both of them.

The mystery should be solved on the fourth birthday of our daughter Miriam. A few days before, Piera brought *Cuor di Mela* (apple hearts) to tea: *The apple hoped to the last that the shortbread would keep both their secrets, but to no avail!* And at the table, she herself had to make a confession:

"You know, I hadn't told my mother that I was working for you, because she wants me to finish my studies quickly, but I also want some space and a little money of my own. The other day, however, she asked me directly where I was going again, and then I didn't have the heart to lie to her and told her everything. But she wasn't angry, she was happy that someone in her circle of acquaintances speaks German again, since she spent her high school years at a boarding school in Switzerland. My mother would like to invite you one day, and I thought it would be a good time next Sunday for Miriam's fourth birthday."

It now turned out that Piera's mother was a well-known Florentine lawyer and she wanted to invite us to her small house by the sea near Pisa. Curious, we drove there the next Sunday. Already on the cypress-lined driveway, our mouths were left open, because the small house presented itself as a spacious villa with a jungle-like garden. Ivy and bougainvillea basked on the Tuscan yellow walls, and orange roses climbed up wrought-iron trellises. The Mediterranean scent of rosemary and mint played around our noses, and the temptation to indulge in idleness, interrupted only occasionally by a glass of red wine, was beguiling in the air.

Piera, again dressed like an Indian snake charmer, met us at the car and escorted us along a shady box hedge to the villa. Through the front door we entered the drawing room, which was furnished in colonial style with a dark-colored mahogany table and leather-covered chairs. Family photos in black and white hung above the open fireplace, evoking the splendor of times past.

"The furniture," Piera explained casually, "is heirlooms from my great-grandfather, who was Italian ambassador to the Ivory Coast." On other dark wood-toned shelves and sideboards were exotic figurines, vases, mugs, jugs, and other keepsakes that came from trips to Africa and Asia.

In the salon, Piera introduced us to her mother Laura, an elegantly dressed middle-aged woman, and her eighty-year-old grandmother Domenica. "She's kind and big-hearted, but a little confused sometimes," Piera apologized in advance. The grandma greeted me effusively with the words "*Che bel tedesco!* ", what a beautiful German man! and gave me two kisses on the cheeks. This made me quite embarrassed, as I had never really impressed women before, if at all, only with my feigned intellectual abilities. Also present was a colorfully dressed Indian family, consisting of father, mother and son, who, as it turned out, were employed as domestic servants. In the presence of the visitors they kept discreetly in the background.

Mother Laura suggested that we first have a small aperitif. The Indian majordomo served a *Mirto,* a Sardinian herb liqueur, for the adults and lemonade, freshly squeezed from their own lemons, for the children. In addition, there was, in a silver bowl, *Batticuori* (heartbeat), of course from Mulino Bianco: *The cocoa dived into a lake full of milk. When it reappeared, it was soaking wet with joy* – life mother, like daughter, I thought to myself.

The rest of the day's program included a visit to the beach. I asked whether we should take bath towels and documents, but mother Laura replied, we should not worry, everything was already provided for. Unfortunately, grandma would have to stay in the house because she couldn't take the sun very well anymore. As we were leaving, she just said to Stephanie, *"Che bel tedesco! "*, what a beautiful German man you have!

After a short walk we reached the sandy beach of Tonfano. Divided into sections, the municipality had given it to private bathing establishments. On each beach lot were about ten rows of sunbeds with umbrellas. Laura and Piera escorted us to a circular spot lined with wooden chairs and shaded by a giant parasol. The spot was in the front row, with a gorgeous view of the Tyrrhenian Sea and the snow-capped peaks of the Apuan Alps rising behind the nearby town of Luca. It was not without pride that Laura reported that her family had been renting that beach spot, sadly not cheap in the meantime, for over twenty-five years. The waiting list for such places is long, she said, which is why the nouveau riche mayor of Florence, a Mr. Trenzi, has only made it to the third row. And doesn't look at the sea, but at the lush bath towels and people's bottoms, the poor bastard!

We made ourselves comfortable in the sun and went for a swim in between while mother Laura procrastinated with a women's magazine on a lounger. When we came back, she meant that it was now time for lunch. I said we'd brought sandwiches, but she smilingly replied that everything was already taken care of. A short time later - and we were beginning to think we had landed in a beach scene from Fellini's *Amarcord* - we caught sight of the Indian family, approaching as if in procession with pots, bowls and jugs and a folding table. With deft hands, they quickly set everything up, and a Tuscan menu now awaited us, with spaghetti al pesto, bistecca with sides, and fruit for dessert, served right on the beach, overlooking the sun, sea, and mountains. To make the movie scenario perfect, Laura served a birthday cake with fresh strawberries for our Miriam, over which she performed jumps for joy.

At the end of the afternoon we returned from the beach to the villa. There the grandmother greeted me again with the words *"Che bel tedesco!"*, in which I was beginning to believe myself now, had not my daughter Sophia rudely inquired: "Is she still quite lucid, the old woman?" In the house the Indian family once more served tea with biscuits, arranged in the drawing-room on the mahogany table in an elegant service by Ginori.

At such times, in the sweltering heat of the summer months, you lose track of time and want only to indulge in life at leisure, I thought, and understood why the Italian upper classes were so adamant about the three-month school holidays from June to September - while less well-off families don't know where to send their children during this period.

Alas, like a summer dream, the day had flown by in a flash, and the farewell was quietly approaching. You just have to have a lucky hand in choosing your nanny, I mused.

"A little snack for the journey home," Piera said, handing us a bag of the incomparable *Pan d'Amore* (love bread):

One day your son will ask you how it happened that he came into the world... You could then tell him about bees, blossoms and pollen... about the stork, or that he was simply lying in the field harvesting cabbages... You could also tell him how it was when mummy and you fell in love!

XII. Italian prehistory

Elba is a Tuscan island in the Mediterranean Sea, originally populated by farmers and fishermen who led an arduous life there. It later provided refuge for a smallish upstart from the neighboring island of Corsica when his pan-European career was shattered and he was due to undergo professional retraining. However, he didn't last long on Elba and from there attempted a career re-entry, which again failed. In the end, he was banished as a long-term unemployed with social benefits to an even more boring island in the South Atlantic, where his life ended, which the Elbanians regret very much for reasons of tourism marketing.

Today Elba is the twentieth German state after Mecklenburg-Vorpommern, Mallorca-Menorca and Gran Canaria-Tenerife, admittedly largely privately owned by members of the moneyed aristocracy of the rich regions of southern Germany. Accordingly, everything is far too well-kept and quiet for Italy, and instead of large hotel castles, mansions, villas and old farmhouses converted into holiday domiciles with stylishly laid-out natural gardens line the slopes going down to the sea. Everything, of course, is neatly fenced and paved with natural stones, in keeping with a Tuscan image that can otherwise only be found in glossy brochures of German DIY stores.

Although living in Florence, we had managed, unlike many Italians, to spend Easter on Elba. Through personal contacts from our German past, we had been able to rent the holiday home of a Munich lawyer. It lay enchanted between maquis and cypresses below the village of Capoliveri in the valley of the small cork oaks, which incidentally was the property of a large industrialist from Augsburg, to whom the Munich enclave was a thorn in the eye. As a matter of routine, a massive barrier separated the whole area from the secondary world, so that no one not belonging to the Nordic dominant culture should stray there.

On our first visit to the town of Capoliveri, we went to a restaurant with the advertising signs of the Erdinger wheat beer brewery emblazoned on its walls. There we took a seat at a free table next to a family with two children. With dark skin and pitch-black hair, they looked typically Italian.

Their table was an impressive sight: Among half-eaten pieces of pizza and empty Coke cans was an impressive collection of dinosaurs, of which I thought I recognized a Tyrannosaurus Rex, a Spinosaurus, an Apatosaurus, and a Velociraptor. This must have been what the Italian prehistoric world once looked like, I thought.

"You know, my doll Emmi has a tummy ache, she had a fight with her sister Elisabeth, and she punched her in the stomach really badly," our four-year-old daughter Sophia addressed the family at the next table in an Italian welcoming statement. Their son then went on a murderous swooping attack with a pterosaur, probably a Quetzalcoatlus, which took off between two cans of Coke.

"You're a funny little chatterbox," the woman from the next table replied, holding her son back with the Quetzalcoatlus.

"No, Emmi really does have a tummy ache," our Sophia insisted angrily.

"I believe you," the woman sought to placate her, adding, "where are you from anyway?"

"From Florence," replied Sophia, who had been born in Italy and was the only one of us who spoke Italian without an accent.

"That's a nice coincidence, we're from Florence too," the woman replied, visibly pleased. "You know, when you came in, I took you, you must excuse me, for German tourists. After all, you have fair skin and blue eyes, and you don't look at all like a true Florentine, but perhaps you have Longobard ancestors. You wouldn't know it, but at this time of year the Germans invade in droves from the north with their fat cars and take over the whole island, you hardly dare speak Italian or make any noise anywhere..."

"I'm the only German in my kindergarten, too," Sophia continued carelessly, "but my friend Ariana is from Cape Verde, and the sisters (meaning the convent sisters who ran the kindergarten) are all from India, except for old Sister Diomira, who has thick glasses because she can't see so well anymore, and she's from Italy."

The woman blushed and turned to us apologetically, "No offense, your daughter speaks like a Florentine, so I thought..."

"Think nothing of it, we are comfortable in Italy and don't always think our countrymen are great either," I replied in my German accent, which sealed the woman's error.

It turned out that our table neighbors were nice people who had rented a holiday apartment via an internet portal from a retired Würzburg notary public who was spending his old age here. However, the conversation never really got going. Sophia and Emmi nevertheless seemed to get on well with the dinos from the next table and didn't even protest when the Quetzalcoatlus got caught in Emmi's hair and committed a massacre on them when he tried to free himself again.

As a farewell, all the dinos paraded past us once again. The Quetzalcoatlus performed aerial tricks, the Spinosaurus wagged its mighty tail joyfully, the Apatosaurus made a manikin on a Coke can, and the Velociraptor offered a leftover piece of pizza with its huge paw. Only the Tyrannosaurus Rex stood scowling off to the side next to the tiramisu, baring his gigantic, brightly flashing teeth and muttering hostilely, "Don't get too excited, I still like eating German tourists best."

Suddenly I realized: "Maybe that's why you went extinct!"

XIII. My first Maserati

When we left the inn after dinner, the primeval still life with the dinos was still circling around in my head, and I only belatedly noticed that something was wedged under the windshield wiper of my car. Although we had not yet encountered the Italian authorities on the island, on closer inspection the something turned out to be a ticket from the local police: thirty-five euros for parking. In fact, I had parked the car in a lot reserved for motorcycles, because the car spaces were occupied by wrecked cars without license plates, so the parking lot looked more like a car cemetery. Which is why I thought, they take liberties with parking here and next to the junk cars my old car wouldn't stand out after all. Disgruntled, I drove the family back to the holiday home. I wondered if the local police would send the ticket to Germany. In Florence they didn't do this, the German license plate number seemed like a carte blanche there, and I had already simply thrown away several tickets. Also the Italian authorities did not check the compliance with the MOT certificate. That's why in Tuscany you often met motorized relics of past times with German number plates, which hadn't been driven in Germany for years. When the police stopped me on a street reserved for buses and taxis in the city center, I pretended to be a tourist and answered cluelessly in English. The policemen should be able to speak that language, but they often don't, for instance when they had got to the police service with the support of a helpful friend of Dad's. But I shouldn't talk so nastily about the Italian officers. For often they have no choice but to sacrifice their grandmother's nest egg in order to purchase the exam questions in the *concorso* (selection test) for admission to the police service, which they then have to learn by heart in painstaking intellectual detail. In the end, the Italian police always let me go with a warning.

But on Elba with so many German tourists? Then I had the idea to ask Bernd from Ingolstadt. We had come across him the other day while walking along the beach, where he ran a diving school during the season. Bernd reported that parking tickets had already been served on several of his customers at home in Germany. And with the processing and translation fees, at least twice the original amount was then incurred.

Thus forewarned, I made my way annoyed to the local police station, which is enthroned like an eagle's nest high up in the center of Capoliveri. I rang the bell at the massive metal gate at the entrance, which immediately unlocked automatically. As I entered, I was taken aback: a heavily made-up model with blond hair, a large bust and tight-fitting clothes approached me and smiled winningly. She reminded me, who admittedly hadn't followed the Italian model market in detail for the last twenty years, of the long-gone Ornella Muti, scantily clad as she graced the BILD newspaper of my youth. Only the dyed blonde hair didn't match. I mused, Ornella must not have been able to decide between a career as a meter maid or a *velina,* meaning *candle.* These are the ladies who bounce around Italian TV shows as living ornaments with heaving breasts and swinging buttocks. And from time to time handing paper and pencil to the naturally male show master, clapping along or performing other services elementary to modern Berlusconi-era television. In fact, the only thing that seemed to stop Ornella from taking part in a casting show (apart from Harald Schmidt's show *The Next Osama Bin Laden,* unfortunately cancelled far too soon) was her smart police uniform.

Pseudo-coolly, I waved the ticket in front of Ornella's eyes and spoke in a firm voice, "I would like to politely request an Easter amnesty from you, I parked my Volkswagen on the parking lot below the church in the motorcycle area because the car spaces were filled with wrecks, and I was promptly warned."

"Yes, that's kind of stupid," she replied sympathetically, "the environmental authority would be responsible for the car wrecks, and we've been wondering why they don't do anything for ages. The parking ticket was issued by my new colleague, you know, we are behind with our monthly amount of tickets to the municipal treasury, so we don't look too closely anymore and take what we get," she said apologetically.

"Couldn't you waive it for me somehow, I'm an old lover of the island after all and I love coming here," I placed an ugly trail of slime in front of Ornella.

"I'd be happy to do that for you," she replied, "but unfortunately the ticket is already registered in our electronic system, and to take it out I'd have to send a written justification to the DA's office, which makes a lot of wind here."

"Well, that's too bad, there must be some way to make this go away? ", I tried to take advantage of Ornella's unexpected willingness to cooperate.

"Ah good, now I think of something," she released the tension in the air. "I could just change the offence category in the system, no one will notice; we'll just put overstaying by less than an hour instead of unlawful parking, it'll only cost nineteen euros - that's the minimum, I'm afraid you can't get any cheaper."

Ornella then handed me a new parking ticket printed out by the computer, which still had the data of a previous driver who had exceeded the parking time - wrong license plate number, wrong car, wrong place and so on.

"But I'm not driving a blue Maserati with Roman plates, I'm driving a German VW Polo, doesn't anyone notice that?", I doubted.

"No, no one cares about that. It's best if you sign here and pay cash right away, then I can archive the process immediately," Ornella replied, now no longer tolerating any objections. I did that right away.

"Don't fret, just don't take Italian bureaucracy so seriously, we don't either, sometimes you are just unlucky, but usually you don't get caught," she regretted my inconvenience.

After these words she stood up, adjusted her lion hair mane with a natural shampoo advertising pose and built her plump model figure in front of me. Then she sucked in my pale face with her sprayed lips, impaled me with her razor-sharp nipples and maneuvered me out the door.

"Have a great holiday! ", Ornella bowed out of my life.

Another case of dormant talents not being used properly in Italy, I thought. Ornella could develop much better, or even disrobe completely, in private television or in politics, perhaps with Silvio himself, than in a barren police station on Elba, where there is nothing to do out of season.

"I unfortunately exceeded the parking time with my blue Maserati in front of the post office and paid a nineteen euro fine for it, I have that in writing here," I explained to the best wife of all upon my return, not without pride.

But she looked at me penetratingly with German perspicacity, patted me compassionately on the shoulder and replied: "Yes, yes, darling, that went very badly with our Maserati, that was supposed to be a belated wedding present from you. And by the way, get dressed properly for once, tomorrow at five o' clock in the afternoon we are invited for tea by Queen Elizabeth II!

XIV. The honorary doctor of the University of Roccaforte

The Decreto Gelmini had hit Italian universities hard. In order to save money, the Berlusconi government's science minister stipulated that only one in four vacant posts could be re-filled. And jobs had been created in abundance at Italian universities in order to adequately serve not only academia but also good friends. So someone came up with the ingenious idea of splitting each course into faculty and department in order to double the administrative structures. The former is responsible for research, the latter for teaching, but since many issues cannot be clearly assigned, in everyday life often no one is responsible for anything. There is also a higher degree of specialization in law than in Germany. In research and teaching, each scientist ploughs through only a tiny area of law, which is why considerably more professors are needed. In theory, at least, because in practice many of them are only present at the university every two or three weeks, knocking off their hourly workload in a few days and having unpaid assistants stand in for them during exams. This allows them to pursue other things - usually not golf or yachting because of the low salaries in the civil service, but running a lucrative law firm in Rome or Milan.

However, I should better be quiet, because I myself had arrived at the southern Italian university of Roccaforte by devious means even before the savings decree. With the aim of alleviating the province's scientific isolation, the regional government had launched an internationalization program that was also intended to attract foreign visiting academics. Internationalization or not, they admittedly had to teach in Italian. But then the university only advertised the positions on its website, which made it unlikely, probably deliberately so, that big names in the field from Oxford, Harvard and Stanford would apply. However, an Italian colleague told me about the job opening, and so I applied and won it brilliantly several times, because I was almost always the only candidate.

The colleagues from Roccaforte accepted me lovingly in their circle and often took me out for above-average meals after my average lectures, such as various kinds of snails, horsemeat and delicate fish specialties. They also invited me out privately. Giovanni, a friendly colleague in civil law, proudly showed me his donkey farm, which kept him very busy - for example, when he received a call during a lecture on bankruptcy law that a donkey had escaped and had to be recaptured as quickly as possible. Or when the donkeys needed extra water in the sweltering summer heat, which he filled in canisters in his private bathroom before the beginning of the working day at the university.

It was during my second year at Roccaforte that, on a beautiful April day before Easter, I found my usually calm colleague Aldo upset in the hallway. Strange news infuriated him. The university had received a mysterious call from Rome asking for a small favor that would surely be returned in one form or another. And because of the tight budget situation, the university would not be averse to granting certain favors.

In Italy's bilateral relations, in fact, an urgent need had arisen for an academic tribute. The leader of the former colonial state of Libya, the famous *King of Kings of Africa,* let's call him Muammar here, had distanced himself from the image of a murdering villain, concluded a peace treaty with Italy and a friendship between men and Berlusconi. As has more recently also become fashionable between would-be dictators from Washington D.C. and London, Downing Street. Italy agreed to pay compensation for the thirty years of occupation and to build motorways. Libya, in return, pledged to supply oil and gas cheaply and, incidentally, to stem the flow of refugees across the Mediterranean to Italy. Older Italians, however, have never forgiven the King of Kings for expropriating and expelling Italians still living in the country after the end of the colonial era decades ago.

But those were *tempi passati,* times gone by. Now, in his second spring, he had taken a liking to making glittering trips to Italy with his court and having himself staged there in photographs and on film, winning over his people. On one visit, in his legendary modesty, he pointed out that he had already received awards from lesser states, including knighthoods, merit crosses, military ranks and honorary doctorates - the latter, however, only from Algeria, Tunisia, Sudan, South Korea, Serbia and Belarus. And that he felt the time had come for the now friendly neighboring country to bestow such an award on him.

The Berlusconi government then used its contacts in the region of Sicily, with which it already had good business relations, for example in buying electoral votes through an internationally known intermediary organization. A Sicilian university was also quick to agree to award Mr Muammar an honorary doctorate in political science. But his response displayed a startling degree of scholarly maturity that, from a legal perspective, made him seem worthy of any award: he indignantly rejected the title of what he called this newfangled gossip science. After all, he said, even Benito Mussolini had received an honorary doctorate from the University of Lausanne only in political science. And he really did not want to put himself on the same level with this utterly failed politician. It should therefore be a serious discipline like law or medicine. This request then brought the University of Roccaforte into play, which has both faculties.

It was precisely this request that Aldo was now dealing with in the internal committees of the university. Along with other opponents, he objected that honorary doctors must have somehow been scholarly active in their field. In fact, there were no legal monographs, textbooks, peer-reviewed articles, commentaries on statutes and decision reviews from the candidate. But someone discovered his so-called Green Book, in which years ago he had put on paper his ideas on state and society somewhere between Marxism and religious fanaticism. [1] His statement that Libya is the only real democracy in the world is well-known from this.

Malicious tongues compared this book with the work of another failed head of state, which also tells of his personal struggle. But a majority in the committees wanted to overlook the minor point that there was nothing legal in it and that the work could perhaps be assigned to the aforementioned gossip science - perhaps because they were already imagining quid pro quos for the small favor. Embarrassingly, no one was found who wanted to give one of the laudations that are customary to pay tribute to the life and work of an honorary doctor. They even asked me, supposedly to give the ceremony a European flair, but I declined with thanks.

Aldo, however, would not give up his resistance and grumbled that the whole thing literally stank to high heaven. However, it was not necessary to go so high. Because someone stole Aldo's old car, an actually unattractive Fiat Punto, a short time later after a committee meeting. The police couldn't solve the crime, but found the car again after a few days in a lonely mountain area. A policeman had gone hunting for wild boar and

---

[1] The Green Paper is available at: www.thegreenbook.eu/dasgruenebuch.pdf

discovered the Fiat by chance in the maquis next to a sheep pen, far from the nearest human habitation. The car was undamaged on the outside, but a look inside revealed the whole disaster: someone had used it to transport live sheep, which are often stolen in the area. And this was done in the interior, which is logistically the easiest way to do it. A connection to the proceedings about the honorary title could never be proven, but Aldo could now well understand how it can already stink on earth.

Mr. Muammar was to receive the award from the hands of the rector shortly before Easter. For this purpose, the honorary doctor-to-be arrived several days before the ceremony with his court of about three hundred people. As a Bedouin from the Libyan desert, he did not stay at the Hilton, but had a respectable tent city erected in the central park. In the main tent, nobly furnished with carpets, divans and crystal chandeliers, the likes of which even trendy camping outfitters do not carry in their assortment, resided the King of Kings himself, together with his favorite wives, the number of which was the subject of various rumors. Noble camels and purebred Berber horses grazed between the tents. Their use on the spot was not immediately apparent to me as a lightweight academic. But then I read in the newspaper that they were supposed to serve as staffage for pompous receptions and to show off the wealth of the host.

The pompous tent city, complete with the king and his horses, camels and favorite wives, was a feast for the local press in the silly season before Easter, which came up with new photo series and reports every day. Only at the edge of the park did a few protesters gain access and hold a foul-mouthed banner in the air: *We already have Berlusconi, we don't need a second dictator!*

My colleague Gaetano also made involuntary acquaintance with the tent city. In one of the Catholic Lenten processions, he was assigned to carry the statue of St. Pio, one of the patron saints of the city. The procession traditionally led through the city park, but the spiritual leaders were apparently not yet aware of its different use this year. So the procession got lost in the tent city and had to start a disorderly retreat, which was not easy for the bearers of the heavy monstrances, canopies and statues of the saints. All in all, it was a rather spontaneous meeting of cultures and religions, as a local newspaper sensitively headlined.

The day before the planned award ceremony, I stopped by the city park out of curiosity. There I saw the King of Kings in person for the first time, dressed imposingly in a white coat with ornaments and military insignia, his face hidden behind large sunglasses and his head covered with a white cap. Curiously, he had surrounded himself with a handsome number of young women, many of them probably students. Elegantly dressed, they formed a ring around the king. It later came to light that the Libyan embassy had hired these women in advance through a hostess service. To them he personally distributed free copies of a book with a fine leather cover, which turned out to be the Koran.

No sooner had I approached the astonishing scene than the king's voice was also heard. He spoke in broken English about religions: "Christianity is in every respect a weak religion that has nothing to say to us. The only true religion is Islam. The accusation that Islam promotes states of God is hypocritical to the core. After all, Christians founded the world's first God-state, which even exists today: the Vatican! Anyone who truly believes in God is a Muslim!"

He then discussed the role of men and women, namely the natural weakness of women due to menstruation and pregnancy and the strength of men, who are spared such adversities and therefore deserve the leading role. Obviously findings of his personal gender research, which modern feminists always like to hear. The young women around him listened in awe. Then he moved on to the topic of childcare, which he had already dealt with profoundly in his Green Paper:

"Separating children from their mothers and stuffing them into day care centers is a process by which they are transformed into something very much like chickens, for day care centers are much like poultry farms into which chickens are stuffed after they have been hatched. Poultry, like the rest of the creatures in the animal kingdom, also need motherhood as a natural phase. Therefore, raising them in nursery-like farms is a violation of their natural growth. Even their meat is closer to synthetic meat than natural meat. Meat from mechanized poultry farms does not taste good and may not even be nutritious because the chickens are not raised naturally, that is, because they are not raised in the protective shade of natural motherhood. The meat from wild birds is tastier and more nutritious because they are raised and fed naturally."

This contribution to human ornithology was also influential in Western Europe. Thus the Libyan king became a role model for politicians in Bavaria, where the monarchy was hastily abandoned after the First World War and is still mourned today. Only a short time ago, the Bavarian ruling party, itself led for years by a wild African ostrich named Strauß, established a so-called herd premium for mothers who do not use external childcare, similar to Mr. Muammar.

Now I should report on the award of the honorary doctorate. But in the end it didn't happen.

Aldo and his friends managed to block the procedure just in time. As a result, it was not officially stopped, but it was allowed to peter out. Just two years later, it sadly became obsolete. A revolution in his own country swept away the King of Kings and drove him from his palace into hiding. There the insurgents tracked him down and cruelly killed him, not entirely unlike the honorary doctor of the University of Lausanne.

After a befitting period of mourning, I loyally offered myself to the university as an innocuous replacement candidate. Unlike the late King of Kings, I have even published legal texts, though admittedly much duller ones than the Green Book. And so hardly anyone would have noticed the honor, let alone taken offense at it. But I was told that honorary doctorates were rarely bestowed honors that should be reserved for the truly great in the field.

And so, to this day, a procedure is pending at Roccaforte University for the award of an honorary doctorate. Donald Trump, who suggests himself as a worthy successor to the late candidate, is unfortunately probably not available. For he has already been nominated for the Nobel Peace Prize.

XV. Men, other cattle and a look in the mirror

„No, that's not how it goes, but not at all," Angelica yelled at my friend Jens, her flat mate. "Don't you have a clue how to do this, you loser? Haven't you ever seen other people do it? What are you thinking? You can't say again: I'm tired and don't feel like going to the movies with you. You know how it works in Italy? I - and not you! - would have to say, bored, I don't feel like going out with you, but you keep asking me and bringing flowers, first tulips, then roses, at first only a few and then more and more and more beautiful, and then after a week I have an espresso with you, bored, of course, and after five minutes I have to leave again to meet my boyfriend, but after two weeks I go to the cinema with you and so on...

I really should have believed my grandma, she always advised me: *Uomini e buoi dai paesi tuoi!* - take men and cattle from your own villages! Well, you are a meathead, Jens, but not from Sicily, but from boring Germany! What a stupid idea of mine to fall for a German political scientist, who writes a doctoral thesis on the history of ideas, but has no idea himself how to behave towards a woman!"

Angelica had talked herself into a frenzy. She was a dark-skinned Sicilian with razor-sharp features, styled curls, and a good figure, wrapped in an understated star-spangled dress. The ancient Greeks had already brought tragedy to Sicily, and the result could still be seen here on the spot two thousand five hundred years later. Angelica was a sociologist, but more than a scientist she looked like the actress Maria Grazia Cucinotta from the beguiling film *Il Postino*. Surrounded by a poignant love story, it relocates the life of the poet Pablo Neruda to Salina, one of the Aeolian Islands off Sicily.

Only after her tirade, Angelica now spotted me in an armchair next to Jens and asked:

"Who's that bore you've got visiting, anyway?"

In fact, she had hit a sore spot. Before the best wife of all took pity on me, I was very popular with the mothers of great women as a candidate for a son-in-law, not least because of my intentions to become a civil servant (for example: "Sabrina, don't you have the time and inclination to take this nice young man out to dinner tonight? Here's fifty thousand lire from Mama for it! "). For them, however, I was only the good buddy to whom one pours out one's heart and a cup of rosehip tea, the gladly called upon grief-processing helper and decision-finding companion, who, however, only comes into question as a partner in a dark dream and, when seen in the light, not even there ("No, Mama, neither").

Jens introduced me to Angelica, "This is Federico, also from Bavaria, he's in the Law Department," adding mischievously, "he's already taken, but maybe you'd like to go to the movies with him?"

In fact, Angelica then asked me, "What are you doing here?"

"I'm writing about the Europeanization of private law," I specified eruditely, but then I immediately regretted it again, because I would rather not make an impression with that.

"What is this stuff?" inquired Angelica suspiciously.

"My thesis is the instrumentalization of private law by the European Union, roughly that Europe uses private law only to enforce its policies, while it doesn't care so much about fair rules between citizens or businesses," I ranted on.

"This is nothing new," Angelica picked apart my scholarly approach of the last ten years. "Every Italian knows that the whole legal system just instrumentalizes citizens. If you pay money to lawyers and courts for fifteen years in a case and then get a decision that does you no good because the parties involved are all dead or bankrupt, what would you call that? Effective legal protection for citizens? But typical lawyers: using words that no one understands, you say things that everyone already knows anyway, and then you use that to pull people's money out of their pockets!"

"Not yet, we still have a scholarship," I wanted to say, but I refrained, because the law track was obviously not going so well. So I tried something else: "Besides law, I also write funny stories, satires about Italy and our life here...".

"What do you mean about my life here too?"

"About the bad morals of the state, for instance. I have a story about a bus driver who once worked in Germany. I had a good chat with him on the way. At first he ranted like a bastard about corruption, but then he cursed the transport department and let me ride for free."

"What's funny about that, it's perfectly normal and happens every day. It doesn't matter if you had to pay one euro eighty for a bus ride or not, nobody really cares! My older brother is also a bus driver down there in Agrigento and always lets his football club ride for free. What do you think he'd get if he made everyone pay. If that's corruption, then the whole of Italy is corrupt. Honestly, I'd be interested to know who'd print such nonsense for you."

"I thought because it's such a pretty contradiction," I defended myself.

"Contradiction, maybe, for people who live in a fantasy world where government employees are paid reasonably and everything works great. But that's not how it is. In Italy, if you get a gift through, how shall I say, a dubious channel, you know what you do? You quickly take it, disappear and keep your mouth shut forever - but you don't write a book about it afterwards! At the most, a few uptight bores, such salon-leftists, latte macchiato greens and Rolex communists, find something like that good. They might read your book while they lounge around in a deck chair next to the fountain in front of their villa and then let the house staff serve them dinner in five courses with champagne. In short, jerks like Jens here," and with that Angelica finally averted her gaze from me, "who wallow in their intellectual worlds but don't know how to handle an Italian woman!"

Postscript: Dear readers, I am extremely embarrassed by these gaffes Angelica has made towards you. It goes without saying that I expect my readers to be of a patriotic republican disposition. Therefore, I would like to apologize to you with the utmost sincerity.

Federico Amadeo Chiodinari

Epilogue: World theatre on the beach[2]

Blazing heat of midday reigned over the Sardinian beach of Costa Rei, an untouched sand dune that nestles endlessly against the sea. Far from any traces of human civilization, it gives off an air of lunar landscape. Somewhere there are supposed to be remains of Greek temples, but they can only be guessed at in the distance. The sky is blue without a cloud, monotonously blue, almost too blue. The sea lies peacefully, content with harmless little waves, and all you see is sand, blinding sand, as far as the eye can see. It doesn't seem like Italy, more like North Africa, where the Sahara reaches the coast.

But like a mirage, people appear. At first dimly in the distance, then closer and closer, until their outlines emerge and their faces become recognizable. A strange company is meeting there: two old gentlemen in silk summer suits, as if they were returning from a rendezvous with Mr. Aschenbach from Death in Venice. Around them, in the midst of many parasols, deck chairs and

---

[2] This chapter is partly based on the story "L'ultima spiaggia della crisi" from Fruttero & Lucentini, Il Cretino in Sintesi, 2002, p. 91, in my translation. The rights are held by the publisher *Mondadori Libri SpA, Milano,* to whom I express my sincere thanks for permission to use it.

beach blankets, a considerable number of women of mature age, all strangely dressed.

The gentlemen introduce themselves as Fruttero and Lucentini, two excellent authors who come from the anti-fascist circles of post-war Turin. They wrote a lot together as a pair of authors - great social portraits hidden in detective stories, but also satires, parodies and glosses that trace the peculiarities of Italians in all their contradictory details.

"These," they explain seriously, "are our crisis ladies, our constant companions. We drove out the king and overcame fascism, and then the communists. But the ladies can no longer be shaken off, they belong to us forever."

The crisis of the heavy industry was an imposing middle-aged appearance with a haggard look, she wore a red blouse and a much too warm long skirt. The crisis of the couple next to her was considerably younger and made a fun-loving impression. She was wearing a gray pantsuit that looked out of place elegant.

They both wandered slowly along the beach at the waterline, leaving marks on the glaring sand that the incoming waves smoothed out in a moment. They seemed absently lost in thought, but in reality their watchful eyes followed every little thing between the countless parasols.

"Look at her acting like a woman of the world!" bemoaned the crisis of the heavy industry.

"Yeah, I'll bet it's gone to her head that everyone's just talking about her," the crisis of the couple crisis scoffed.

They met the crisis of the automobile industry with a half-hearted salute, nodding at them from above. But just a few meters away, surrounded by a collection of admirers, sat the crisis of the political left.

"It's baffling to me that she isn't ashamed of herself, at her age. She's in her second spring, if not her third or fourth."

"And yet she's still there, holding court, with her myriad wrinkles and folds."

"Unbelievable! You know, she was born the same year as my grandmother, just a little later than the crisis of the Mezzogiorno."

Now a nondescript little woman with dark skin came along the way. Bent under heavy loads, the immigration crisis rattled the beach, hawking goods of all kinds, from towels to diving goggles to magazines. But no one seemed interested in her.

There approached at a run a bare-breasted adolescent in the splendor of her youth, her long legs flinging forward with nonchalant agility. She did not dignify the crisis of the heavy industry and her colleague of the couple a glance.

"Was she just pretending now, do you think?"

"No, no, she's so haughty she doesn't see anyone but herself. The birth crisis is the undisputed star of the beach, having been voted Miss Sandcastle two summers in a row!"

"Well bravo, and then a big wave came and washed them away?"

"Give me a break, she has overtaken the crisis of confidence, the crisis of credibility, the crisis of employment, the crisis of public transport and then the crisis of public broadcasting."

"And what about the crisis of the political institutions?"

"She didn't participate at all, she's too stuck up and snobby."

Then, anxiously, an old lady in a high-necked black bathing suit rose from her snow-white terrycloth towel and made an effort to start a conversation.

"Go away, go away, don't stop!"

The two smiled affably at her, but at the same time quickened their pace and left her on the spot, undone.

"This is the crisis of religious vocations."

"For God's sake, that old-fashioned spinster!"

But when they saw the big four-sided tent standing there, away from the plebeian mass of parasols squeezed together like sardines in oil, they remained undecided.

"Do you think we shouldn't pay our respects?"

"She's still the ruler, isn't she?"

"Agreed, but let's just stay a little while, and then let's get out of here!"

The crisis of values was enthroned in a sprawling bast chair, exuding a triumphant aura. A stone-aged lady who had ruled the beach since time immemorial. She extended her wizened hand of many rings to the two newcomers and introduced them to the other guests of the day: the crisis of the currency, the crisis of the publishing industry, the crisis of the secret services, the crisis of historic city centres, and the crisis of sex, who came forward, clad in a motley scrap of cloth that really no longer concealed the slightest thing.

"Want a slice of pizza?"

"Gladly!"

The offer came from a nondescript woman with grey hair tied into a bun, elongated face, and an oversized kimono that looked like an apron.

"And who would that be, her chambermaid?"

"But don't you recognize her? It is the crisis of satire!"

"No way, I don't believe it! The last I heard of her was that she had severe paralysis and could only move her left little finger."

"That's true, but she had a physical therapist treat her. And the twenty sessions with him counted against her four years' sentence in purgatory. So she quickly returned, recovered and had a lift. Now she has discovered Matteo Salvini,

Björn Höcke, Donald Trump and Boris Johnson. With them she hangs around everywhere, sticks her nose into everything, and so she always finds someone to serve her."

"But she can barely manage to stay on her feet, poor thing! Honestly, one can only feel sorry for her!"

"Tell me about it, she's just so tiny and inconspicuous.... All you have to do is clap your hands firmly and she'll disappear, retire to her bower and not show her face again for the next ten years. Shall we offer her a little aperitif?"

The crisis of immigration had a bottle of spumante and other high-proof drinks ready in a cooler that she dragged behind her next to her countless bags and boxes. She placed three glasses on a silver tray, poured, and handed them to the bystanders. The crisis of heavy industry beamed at her fellow couple, and they clinked their glasses together and shouted, "Long live satire!"

No sooner had they said that than the smiles froze on their lips. A whirring sound began, which grew stronger and stronger until a thunderous noise congealed them all. Lightning flashed across the firmament, and abruptly the beach darkened. Bathed in blinding light, a chariot with twelve steeds and apocalyptic riders chased through the sky. In it sat, in a golden gown, a monstrous fairy with a hateful, all-devouring gaze: Corona. The crisis of satire pulled out a notebook before she was struck down by lightning, the crisis of values hurriedly buried herself in the sand and covered hers head, the crisis of religious vocations dragged herself kneeling into the water, spread her arms and sank. And the crisis of couplehood, the crisis of birth, the crisis of trust, and the crisis of political institutions stammered, "Take what you want, you can have it all from us, we never want to be crisis again. Only spare our beautiful old Italy, the Italy of Boccaccio!"

About this book

In the footsteps of the Decameron, this little book describes the chaotic and sympathetic adventures of a German student at a European university in Florence. A stone's throw away from Boccaccio, the Italians despise their state and all authorities, but hold high shrewdness, cunning and sensuality. The students are infected by this and become heroes and victims of satire themselves. The series opens with a bus driver who mercilessly exposes the deplorable state of affairs in the country, but is unexpectedly generous when it comes to selling tickets. No less astonishing is the ponderous local police, who do not prosecute petty criminals, but creatively invent discounts on parking tickets. Meanwhile, there is a shipwreck off Elba under the influence of alcohol and a volcanic eruption in Sardinia in which Silvio has a hand. At the climax of the satirical carnage, a South Tyrolean landlord deceitfully throws Italian beau out of his mountain lodge, while two German academic lightweights indulge in vegetarian honey-tonguing. An overzealous conductor who mutilates himself at a concert is no longer noticeable.

But love flies above everything, only here it writes stories of a different kind: a troubadour tries in vain to beguile his sweetheart with his singing, and in the process falls off the roof of her house. A couple of students living at home have to make do with their father's car, which a precariously employed person covers with newspapers beforehand. A Spanish-Swedish couple teaches their pale-skinned offspring a language otherwise only known from Nazi films. And a four-year-old finds out under strange circumstances why the dinosaurs on Elba got extinct.

But the fun is over when the spurned Sicilian beauty Angelica appears, who wants to throw all the stories in the bin and you, poor and perhaps innocent readers of the book, right after them. Boccaccio would be delighted with his descendants, were it not for the hateful fairy Corona at the end, who as the new plague wants to wipe out old Italy. All of this happened in some way, but none of it is true!

www.ingramcontent.com/pod-product-compliance
Lightning Source LLC
LaVergne TN
LVHW010601160826
845677LV00013B/3201

9798417155482